M000017804

STARK TALES

An Anthology

Compiled & Edited by Mela Saylor

Eleni Byrnes, Assistant Editor

A Publication of the Greater Canton Writers' Guild, Inc.

The Greater Canton Writers' Guild, Inc.

All rights reserved.

No part of this publication may be reproduced, stored in a retrieval system, or transmitted in any form or by any means, electronic, mechanical, photocopying, recording or otherwise, without prior written permission of the publisher.

With the exception of "Boilers", these stories are works of fiction. Names, characters, places, and incidents are either the product of the author's imagination or, if real, used fictitiously. Any resemblance to actual events, locales, or persons, living or dead, is entirely coincidental.

Cover photography by Jean Trent Beyond the Images Photography.
Layout and design by Jean & Steve Trent © 2019
Website: www.beyondtheimages.com
https://www.facebook.com/beyondtheimagesphotography/
email: beyondtheimagesphotography@gmail.com

Front cover photograph by Jean Trent, Beyond the Images. The first clock in this photo is a Herschede Modern Tall Case Grandfather.

Printed and bound in the United States of America

Published by The Greater Canton Writers' Guild, Inc.
P.O. Box 8381
Canton, Ohio 44711-8381

Second Paperback Edition
ISBN: 978-1-09832-513-8
Copyright 2019 the Greater Canton Writers' Guild, Inc.
Compilation © 2019 the Greater Canton Writers' Guild, Inc.

Contributing Authors

Alford, William	"Taken Out"
Byrnes, Eleni	"Fly in the Ointment"
Dine, Benjamin	"Forwards from Backward"
Klink, Edward	"Applejack"
	"Buggers"
Luikart, Ron	"Episode at the Palace"
	"Charles S. Price"
	"Lamy's"
	"The Mission"
Saylor, Mela	"At the Symphony"
	"Back at the Clock Shop"
	"Discovery after the Whirlwind"
	"Sundown at the Cemetery"
	"The Return of Time"
	"Time Amok"
	"Time Flies at 8:20"
	"Twilight of Time"
Totten, Caroline	"Mrs. Shymanski"
Trent, Jean	"A Dance in the Dark"
	"Boilers"

Contents

Preface

This book began as an exercise to see if a group of disparate writers across a myriad of genres could write a story together.

We started out with an idea from a play on words and created characters that would move in and out of our stories, essentially tying them together into one cohesive unit. This particular story line allowed everyone to write in their own genres and preferred time periods.

Every effort has been made during the lengthy editing process to keep each contributing writer's own voice and writing style intact.

This labor of love has been a long, slow process – the intermingling of ideas, inspiration, magic, and hard work. But nothing good comes easy. We hope you enjoy reading this as much as we did in its creation.

Chapter 1: Time Flies at 8:20

Written by Mela Saylor

Jackson Township, August 20th, 1921

Ohio, United States

Sun and shadows flickered as unusual clouds swept over the empty farmland. In the middle of a cornfield in what would eventually become Jackson Township, a shop from a small strip mall appeared and disappeared as erratically as the clouds that caused the flickering shadows over the ground. The land shuddered the moment the strip mall finally materialized with a sonic boom, and the sole occupant, now in his early teens, opened the door and stuck his head out. His clock shop sat in the middle of a cornfield; the almost ripe stalks towered over his head obstructing his view.

"Jonas, NOOOO!" he yelled at the sky. He slammed the door, and frantically began tearing his place apart, clock by ticking clock.

The last thing Thomas Berg remembered was the outer bell in Jonas Freake's shop ringing right before Jonas and his entire shop disappeared. There was that thing that Jonas had said, though, as he waved his arms above his head. His stomach lurched as he was catapulted into time and within a matter of seconds, he stood in a small shop amid hundreds of ticking clocks. ***What just happened and what did Jonas do?***

Stunned, Thomas forgot he was holding the vials Jonas had given him and dropped them. Before his eyes, before he could react, two silver-white insects, the timeflies, according to Jonas, flew off screeching into the recesses of his clock shop. ***His clock shop?*** Thomas looked around overwhelmed with all the clocks and his strange new surroundings – and the sound they all made together. *What had Jonas done to him? How did he do that?*

Norway
1961

"Come here, I want to show you something you'll never see again in your life." Jonas Freake whispered to Thomas as he looked around his shop - Freake and Monter's Emporium, to make sure his associate Meester Monter was out on an errand and no one could hear him. Thomas pushed his sense of deja vu away as he reluctantly followed Jonas to the backroom.

In the farthest corner of his shop behind some strategically placed grandfather clocks, there was an antiquated wood door sealed with chains and a lock. He removed a key from inside his somewhat medieval voluminous black robe and unlocked it. The door creaked and groaned in protest when forced open. Thomas was surprised the old man had the strength to open it.

Once inside, Jonas flipped a light switch and electricity flooded the area. This secret room looked like a long narrow cave, with single light bulbs hanging every fifteen feet down its length. Thomas looked around in amazement.

"No electricity out in the shop but just in here? Really?"

"What? I wasn't born in the 14th century, you know. Maybe the 15th, I really don't remember now." He muttered as he shuffled toward the back of the dimly lit room. The low-wattage light bulbs hanging down the center of the ceiling over a long wood table cast menacing shadows in every crevice. "I've got to see what's going on in this place." He grumbled as he shuffled around in his robes.

As Thomas followed Jonas deeper into the back of the room, the wood plank floor stopped, and the dirt floor began. Cobwebs hung from everywhere. Seemingly random objects were in rows on the rough-hewn shelves that lined the walls. Batteries, shoes, art supplies, seed packets, dolls, and cookbooks, to name a few. The arrangement appeared haphazard. And on the floor were an odd assortment of windows, furniture, and bags of specialty clays he had to step over. On the shelving at the back of the room stood a row of large old books. Jonas started moving the books around in order to stick his arm behind them. He was looking for something he kept hidden, even in this secret room. Thomas started looking around.

"What's this?' Thomas warily eyed a large clear sealed container the size of a wine vat that contained dark swirling clouds in it. If he didn't know better, they looked angry.

"Be careful." Jonas steered Thomas away from the huge clear container. "That is full of bad ideas that my daughter collects from the minds of mankind. She takes them out of circulation."

"Cool. And what's in those books you have there?" Thomas wondered about the old man's mental state because of the moth-eaten robes he wore and his acting as if he was a sorcerer. Jonas almost had Thomas convinced of that except for

9

the bright white tennis shoes Thomas saw peeking out from under Jonas's robe. Still, he humored the lonely old guy.

"This book," Jonas said as he held it reverently, "is a book of wasted talents, and the other one a compendium of every thought ever thought by everyone who has ever lived on this planet." Jonas put the books down and rolled one of his sleeves up to reach further back into the recesses of the shelving. Hidden behind the books were two large glass cylinders, about an inch wide and eight inches tall, with domes on both ends. Thomas had to squint in the dim lighting to see what Jonas pulled out.

"Um, what's in those things?"

"These are from Pandora's trunk of curses."

"Pandora? I thought it was a box? – curses?"

"Eh – potato – potahto." Jonas shrugged. "Never mind that. These creatures are called timeflies – both male and female here. This is the ultimate in time pieces because they can control time. These are the switches and anyone who holds these controls the future – or can really mess with it. I just came into possession of these two creatures again".

"Again? You mean you lost them once?"

"Some French guy came snooping around years ago. Jules Hearn? Or was it Verne? I don't remember the last name, but he was the nosiest guy ever. He stole the timeflies from me for a while and took them for a joy ride. Anyway, it doesn't matter. My daughter was able to retrieve them."

"Oh!" Thomas brightened up considerably when he heard Jonas had a daughter. "You have a daughter? What's her name?" Jonas stopped in mid-sentence and glared at Thomas. One long bony finger came out and he pointed it at Thomas.

"My daughter? Karma – and you don't want to mess with her. At all."

At that moment, the door to the outer shop jangled open and a voice boomed.

"Jonas! Where are you?"

Jonas paled and took a deep breath.

"Demonico - that devil. Oh crap." He looked intently at Thomas and whispered.

"It is imperative you protect these for me. I'll bring you back when it's safe – so ***stay put!***"

"Jonas! I know you're here!" the voice was coming closer.

Jonas threw his hands in the air and fiercely whispered "Temptation-Time-Tangents - Be gone!"

August 1921 – Lake Cable, Ohio

And now the timeflies had disappeared into the recesses of this new place. He had to get them back before anything else happened.

At the same time in Lake Cable

"Did you feel that?" Dorothy looked up from her sketchbook and swatted Reginald away from nuzzling the back of her neck. It was a gorgeous August weekend and Dorothy, her boyfriend Reginald, and their two engaged friends, Edward, and Elizabeth, decided to camp out for the weekend. They were also making their own brew of moonshine away from the curious eyes of the town busybodies.

Large cumulous clouds sailed by in a stiff wind overhead in the cerulean sky while Elizabeth and Edward took a walk down to the stream to get water. Dorothy wanted to lie on the warm ground with her sketchbook and drink in the sun. She kept swatting Reginald's advancements away with an errant hand.

"Why darling," Reginald murmured behind her ear, "are you telling me you felt the earth move when I kissed you?"

The next tremor wiped the smile from his face and knocked his glass of gin over from their illegal still that they had been producing all morning on their campout.

The breeze changed direction at the second tremor and the clouds shot out overhead from a central location emulating the tremors they had just felt.

Edward and Elizabeth ran back from the creek panting and excited.

"Did you feel that? Did you *HEAR* that?" Edward's face was red with excitement.

"Was that what I thought it was? An earthquake HERE? In Ohio of all places?" Reginald jumped up from the picnic blanket he and Dottie had been on and helped Dottie up.

"But it couldn't have been – did you see the clouds with the last boom? Something else had to have occurred." Dottie was fumbling with her sketchbook and pencils trying to collect her stuff.

"Of course it was – and we are witness to it! I've got to find the epicenter. Do you have any idea how grand that would be for me to write a paper on that? It was pretty loud so it can't be too far from here." Edward kept prattling on about the new paper he was going to write as he and Elizabeth started breaking down camp.

"I gather that to mean we are all going with you. What about the still? We can't tote that around with us, and what if someone finds it? Do you have any idea the kind of trouble we'd be in? And our reputations? We'd be ruined, I say." Reggie looked around the clearing.

"We can hide the still in the thicket over there. It should be safe for a day or so. Let's just finish what we have right now- cheers!" Edward poured another glass for himself and gave his fiancé, Elizabeth the rest. She giggled.

"And now we're off on another grand adventure! To us!"

While the four of them took off due south across the field and forests to what they deemed was the epicenter of the earth tremors, Dottie's stomach started rolling. Something wasn't right and she couldn't put her finger on it.

It took the four of them several hours as Edward was in the lead with his ever-present compass to get across the many wheat fields. Elizabeth and Dottie were getting increasingly tired and irritated with the men walking and talking amicably in front of them in the humid August heat. The afternoon sun beat down on them unmercifully. The heat didn't seem to bother the men.

Dottie was purposefully slowing them down any way she could. With every step she took she felt a sense of dread – of déjà -vu – that she couldn't figure out.

"Dottie! Elizabeth! Hurry up!" Edward turned and glared at the two women who were slowing his progress. He wanted to be the first on the scene of what he was sure would be an incredible find.

"How do you even know what you're looking for, Edward?" Elizabeth snapped. "I didn't sign up for a hike – and we're not exactly dressed for one either! Look at us!" Edward and Reginald stopped in their tracks to turn and look at the women with a blank look on their faces. "What?" They shrugged their shoulders and kept walking.

"Listen – there's a small woods up ahead which we're going to go through. We can take a short rest when we get to it, okay?" As he kept trudging ahead while talking to the women, they had to run to catch up with the determined Edward to hear what he was saying.

"Plus, there's probably a small stream of sorts, don't you think, Ed?" Reginald, trying to be helpful, looked back at the women he was trying to placate. The last thing he needed was an irate Dottie. She could be a handful when irritated, he discovered. "You girls will be able to fill the canteens there, too." Dottie smiled at him, then turned and rolled her eyes at Elizabeth.

"One more wheat field to go, Dottie, then we can sit down. What a day, huh?"

"This is certainly not what I expected to be doing, that's for sure. "Dottie stood still for a second and shook her skirt, trying to cool off.

The woods loomed ahead of them and as soon as the four of them got inside under the trees, they felt an immediate drop in temperature. The girls found the closest log and sat down, throwing their gear on the forest floor.

"That's it, Edward. We'll wait for you right here. Hear me? We're not getting up." Elizabeth was adamant, and Dottie just glared at the two men. This, it was apparent to her, was turning into a wild goose chase.

"We – we'll go now – look for a source of water and fill up the canteens for you." Reginald smiled at the women as he pulled Edward away from them. Edward could be annoying at times. *Besides, the women really needed to cool off, literally and figuratively*, he thought, chuckling to himself.

"What's so blasted funny, chap?" Edward scowled. "You know we're losing time, don't you?"

"We'll all be leaving here soon enough." They made their way through some underbrush.

"How do you know that?'

"Because this is the woods. Nice and cool. Damp, rotting wood. Bug heaven. And Dottie and especially Liz, don't like bugs." Reginald turned to Edward and smiled, tapping his head by the temple.

"Ah, brilliant! We better get those canteens filled, then we can be off."

The men soon found a stream and were able to fill all four canteens with water and were halfway back to where they left the women when they heard screaming.

Reginald and Edward were out of breath by the time they got to Dottie and Elizabeth. The screaming had since stopped. They found the women still seated on the fallen log, but this time they were holding a cat. Dottie was giving it some of the food they had packed.

"Look, Edward, we found this poor little cat in here." Elizabeth looked up at him and smiled "Isn't it wonderful?" Edward gave her a pained look; he was still trying to catch his breath from his mad sprint through the woods. He put his hand on his chest.

"You were screaming, my dear."

"Oh, yeah." And giggling, Elizabeth told Edward and Reginald how she and Dottie found the cat rustling in the bushes thinking it was a wild animal.

"And that's why we're adopting her and taking her home with us. Isn't she adorable? What shall we name her, Dottie?"

"Hmm – she has the coloring of my great Aunt Cora. Let's call her Cora Beasty."

"Why Beasty?"

"Because we found her in the woods and thought she was a little beast."

~~

An hour later they saw a building in the middle of John Bell's northernmost cornfield. No one else would have seen it at this point in the growing season since it was August and the corn was ten feet high already. Dottie was expecting to see something and noticed it first.

"Hey – look over that direction!" she pointed west to where they were standing, having stopped for a rest and canteen break.

"Where?" Elizabeth shielded her eyes against the late afternoon sun.

"Right over the last rise against that copse of trees. You can see the roof from here." Reginald squinted into the setting sun.

They gathered around, staring at the place.

"Who on earth would build here? It's in the middle of a blasted cornfield?"

"This doesn't look right." Elizabeth stopped to readjust Cora in her arms.

"Let's go check it out – maybe whoever lives there can tell us more about that earthquake. Surely they had to have felt that." Edward was positive they were getting closer to his epicenter.

Another fifteen minutes marching through the cornfield lead them directly to the building, but they stopped short of going to the door. A single two-story building was sitting in the middle of the cornfield, corn growing a minimum of ten feet high all around, but although it was a single building, there was a rectangular imprint with crushed cornstalks all around it. Everything in that perimeter had been flattened. They walked around the area and studied it.

"What do you think happened, Edward? Could this possibly be related to the tremors we felt?" Reggie shook his head and murmured.

"Very peculiar, I say." He glanced at the building and found Dottie and Elizabeth peeking in the front window, not being able to suppress their curiosity. "Hey there! Get away from the window!"

They wouldn't budge

"SHH!" Elizabeth turned to Reginald. "Take a look in here – there's nothing but clocks and clocks! I've never seen so many clocks in my life! Who could possibly need all those clocks?"

"Perhaps this is a clock shop?" Reginald jockeyed for a position at the window.

"Maybe – but in the middle of a cornfield?" Elizabeth observed, glancing at Edward briefly. "Very odd if you ask me. Take a good look around here – there's no road, not even a path, and no vehicles of any kind, not even a horse. It's like this place, just landed. Something is wrong with this picture."

"Let's just leave right now." Dottie pleaded "I've got a bad feeling about this, okay?" Her left eye was twitching.

"I wonder if there's running water in there?" Elizabeth asked.

"It sure looks a lot cooler in there, don't you think?'

While all this was happening on the outside of the shop, Thomas was inside crawling around on his hands and knees looking for the timeflies that had gotten away. He was searching every inch of the place, including the clocks.

Thomas was getting tired, very hungry, weak, and cranky – and then he heard voices. They seemed to be getting closer, so he stopped to try to listen to what they were saying, fervently hoping it would be in English so he could at least communicate with whoever was out there. He scooted closer to the window, head down. Whoever was out there sounded like they were on the other side of the window he was currently crouched under. It was English they were speaking! Excitedly, he popped his head up to see who they were.

As Elizabeth and Dorothy had their noses to the glass and were looking intently through the window trying to figure out why the shop was there, a pale frightened face popped up from the other side. Startled, they jumped back, screaming. The man on the other side screamed.

"Someone is in there!"

When Thomas realized that those people outside were going to want to come in, he ran to the door to keep it shut. The last thing he wanted was to let those two insects out. He'd never get them back if they were let out.

"Is he okay?" Edward asked Dottie as he helped Elizabeth off the ground. She clutched the cat. "Go see if he's okay, please, Dottie."

Dottie stammered. "No" She was adamant. "I h-have a bad feeling."

"Oh just open the door and see if he's okay – we'll be right behind you." Reginald said.

Dottie tugged on the door and it wouldn't budge.

"No – no – no!" Thomas was on the other side trying to keep the door shut but everyone outside thought he was in distress. When the door finally opened, six silvery white insects flew out, furious and screeching. Elizabeth and Dottie stopped in their tracks to cover their ears. The cat jumped out of Elizabeth's arms and ran into the building. No one noticed.

It was almost dusk at the time, so the insects were visible because they emitted a light similar to that of lightening bugs.

"Nooo!" Thomas stood there and cried watching them disappear into the night sky.

"The flies! You let them out." Thomas turned on Dottie accusingly. "What have you done you little twit? Please tell me this is all some kind of bad trip." Thomas hung his head and closed his eyes.

"Huh?" Dottie blanched thinking, *I've done this before?* Elizabeth leaned toward Edward and whispered.

"Isn't he, like fourteen? And talking like that! What's a 'bad trip'?"

A puzzled look crossed Thomas's face and he became quiet upon noticing his visitors clothing. He looked at them and whispered, "What year is this?"

"1921" Edward stepped up to Thomas and looked at his clothing.

"This is America, right?" Thomas asked.

"Yes. And where do you come from?"

"Chicago, 1961. Bu-but I wa-was in Norway on family business when this happened." Thomas spread his arms wide encompassing the entire shop.

The girls' eyes were as wide as saucers upon hearing Thomas's story.

"Who did this to you?" Dorothy finally spoke up.

"A sorcerer named Jonas with white tennis shoes." Thomas spit the words out.

20

"I have a question for you here, chap," Reginald announced.

"What are tennis shoes?" Thomas asked.

"No, but good question," Reginald continued. "Why aren't any of your clocks working? Are they broken?"

"You're right!" Thomas cocked his head to the side, listening. All he heard were the katydids outside. "The clocks were driving me to distraction while I was looking for Jonas's insects. And then the door opened, and the insects left – that's when the clocks stopped!" He looked at the frozen clocks. The time on every one of them had stopped at 8:20 pm. His eyes flew to Dottie sitting there. "You!" He pointed at her. "You did this!"

"I-I'm sorry." Dottie blinked rapidly, trying not to cry. Reginald put his arm around her.

"Edward and I told her to open the door – *we* heard you yelling in here and thought you needed help. Sorry, chap.

~

It was almost morning by the time introductions were made and many questions were answered. Weary, they all sat in stunned silence in a circle on the floor of the clock shop pondering the brevity of the situation and the certain calamity if those flies were not recovered.

"I still cannot believe how quickly those insects managed to procreate in the short time it took to find them." Dottie was incredulous. Edward could only look at her and grin. And for that he received an elbow in his ribs from Elizabeth.

"Don't." She looked him in the eyes and rolled hers.

21

Thomas sat, bleary eyed and wondering if the place had an upstairs and a bed. Disaster or not, he needed sleep.

"I've never seen such a creature before. Truly, they are magical." Everyone agreed with Reginald's assessment.

"How would one go about catching those timeflies – is that what you call them?"

"Yes – and apparently they're dangerous in the wrong hands. I surmise that's why I've been sent here with them." He looked at Dottie sternly and shook his head. "You need to retrieve them."

"How am I supposed to do that?"

The shop and land shuddered once, and a slip of paper floated down from the large light in the ceiling fan above them. Thomas looked heavenward as he grabbed it. He read it aloud.

"Go find Thomas in the year 2017. He will have something that will bring them back." An irritated Thomas looked heavenward again and shouted at Jonas. The light blinked.

"Jonas! What the blazes are you doing in there? And I don't see how we're doing to get them back now – your flies could be anywhere by now. Can't your daughter get them back again? Ask her!" And once again a slip of paper floated down. Everyone sat there stunned into silence watching Thomas converse with an all-seeing entity from another time. Edward grabbed the second paper, blinked once, and read aloud:

"We're not telling her. Don't mess with Karma. Tell Dottie to get bit first."

"So where do we go?" Elizabeth was bewildered with the bizarre turn of events, but so glad she didn't have to get near one of those shrieking insects.

"We can try those woods we passed through on our way here," Edward said. "They seem to be a bug haven."

Dottie got up from her sitting position on the floor and dusted herself off. "Ok, let's get this over with. I just want to go home and get a bath at this point."

The four of them ended up in the woods where they found Cora the cat.

"This place looks like it's dark enough to find any of those time flies should they be here." Edward remarked as he looked around.

"I don't want to touch those things. I won't." Elizabeth was starting to panic. "This is almost just like a dream I had when I was little – bugs and bugs flying at me – and then me falling into them and flying!" She looked up at Edward, pleading. "Why can't I wait with Thomas at the shop? I can take care of Cora."

"My dear, we don't know if that place will be there when we get back You don't want to go with the old man to some place in Northern Europe, do you? Chances are you won't speak the language, besides," Edward looked over the summer dress she was wearing, "you're not dressed for it – hmm?"

"And for all we know," Reginald added "that shop could just go – like that!" He snapped his fingers in front of her face. Elizabeth jumped.

"Do we all remember what we're to say when we get one?" Edward asked the group. Everyone nodded and spread out slightly except for Elizabeth, who was clinging to Edward, refusing to let him leave her side.

"Shh!" Edward hushed them, pointing to Dottie a few yards away. She was standing by a thicket with sunlight streaming down from the canopy. Within that errant sunbeam a thousand dust motes danced and glittered. One sole time fly danced with them. Dottie slowly reached an open hand just outside the sunbeam and after a slight hesitation the timefly landed on it. Then she gently closed her hand and said aloud what she had been told directly by the wizard Jonas: "First bite – I'll hold tight, so take me where you might make things again right and rectify."

Dottie looked up at her friends. Nothing happened. Surprised, she opened her hand only to discover the time fly had disappeared!

"Where'd it go?" Reginald looked around.

"I've no idea."

And just then, Dottie heard music. She turned to her friends with a huge smile.

"Do you hear that? It's the most beautiful music I've ever heard." Then she felt the tremors begin in her feet, similar to a tingling one would get when their feet fell asleep and were waking up.

"Oh –" Then Dottie disappeared with a pop.

"What the deuce?" Reginald, who had been closer to Dottie, blinked and rubbed his eyes.

"Where did she go, Reggie? Get her back! What music was she talking about?" A terrified Elizabeth was not going to let Edward disappear on her like that. She clung on to him tighter.

"Wherever she's gone, we have to go too." A determined Reginald said. He looked at Edward and Elizabeth clutching each other and smiled. "Think of this as something else you can write about later, chap."

Then he walked up to the brush with the dancing motes and held out his hand. Another timefly came out of nowhere and landed on his hand. He said what Thomas had him memorize and as he disappeared, Edward ran to the same spot, dragging Elizabeth with him.

"Elizabeth – you HAVE to – we'll go together, but we've got to do this now!" Edward grabbed her hand and forcibly opened it. When a timefly appeared and landed on her hand, he covered it with his own hand.

"Look at me, Elizabeth." Edward commanded." Say it with me, Liz" And they did.

Edward and Elizabeth stood alone together in the silent woods and looked into each other's eyes.

"Do you feel it beginning, Liz? Are your feet vibrating?"

"I'm frightened. And I hear the music, too. They're singing. What is it, Edward?"

"I think we're about to be on our way!"

"Where are we going? Please hold on to me." Elizabeth started to sob.

"Why, we're going off on an adventure!" As Edward held Elizabeth in his arms and bent down to kiss her, they disappeared in the twinkling of an eye.

Chapter 2: Twilight of Time

Written by Mela Saylor

Everhard Rd.

August 2017

Astrid was on her way home from the writers' group meeting that night when she was sitting at the stop lights at Everhard Road and Whipple when a timefly flew into the windshield just as she was coming to a stop.

CRACK! At first, she thought it was a small stone that had hit the car. Then she looked closer. It turned and looked right back at her and let out a small shrill sound and flapped the one wing that wasn't caught. Stunned, she took off her glasses and looked at it closer through the window, not believing what she was seeing.

"A timefly? You've got to be kidding! The world is going crazy," she thought as she put her car in park and got out at the intersection amid the honking of cars around her. The fly lay stunned on her windshield and had one of its legs caught under a wiper blade. The light had just turned green and uncaring of the commotion and mild congestion she was causing, she gingerly grabbed it by one wing as she lifted her wiper blade off of it. She studied it again. It looked a little different from the artist rendering of these renowned insects in their Big Book of Dark History that she was in possession of, but she was almost positive that that was what this creature was. She got back in the car holding it in one hand and drove to the nearest parking lot in order to find a container in her bag she could put it in temporarily. A storm was brewing west of the Belden Village area where the car was parked, probably in nearby Lake Cable, she surmised. Lightening flashed in the sky.

"That figures." She looked at the darkening sky taking a deep breath. Trembling, she took out her cell phone and dialed. "Miranda? You're not going to believe what I ran into on the way home."

Chapter 3: Episode at the Palace
Written by Ron Luikart

Canton, Ohio
2017/1926

Ed Smith exploded out of the front door of the Grand Hotel in Canton. His skin from the neck up was a vivid red. His hands were clinched in fists so tight that his fingernails cut into the palms of his hands, but he didn't feel any of that pain. He sucked in great gulps of air. His heart seemed ready to jump out of his chest, but he didn't feel that either. He saw a near-by trash can and lashed out at it with his right foot and sent it and its contents cascading onto the sidewalk and into the street. He paced quickly up and down stomping his feet with each step.

Soon another man came out of the hotel and stood for a moment watching Ed. After the trash can banged to the sidewalk, he approached him and put a hand on Ed's shoulder.

"Ed, Ed! You need to settle yourself and get some control."

Ed looked at the man with his wide eyes.

"Tom, you and I came all the way from Houston, right?"

"Sure. Of course we did."

"You and I both have PHDs in geology, right?

"Yeah. So?"

"Well explain to me how a long-haired, braided pig-tail, hippy type from the 70's, living in some berg named Dover can lecture and tell me all about how fracking works."

"Listen, Ed."

"I mean, after all, it is 2017!" Ed interrupted.

People on the sidewalk stopped and began to stare.

29

Tom grabbed Ed by the shoulders and shook him.

"Ed, shut the hell, and listen!"

Ed's countenance began to change, and his breathing slowly returned to normal. He looked at Tom.

"Sorry," he said, "guess I was a real jerk."

"Yeah, you were."

"Still, here we are trying to make their lives better, and they get all upset about it."

"It's change, Ed, nobody likes change. Our first job is to show them how this change and this new technology is beneficial to everybody."

Ed took a deep breath. Paused. "Alright," he said.

"Listen we have a couple of hours before the next meeting. Why don't you just take a walk, have a drink, and see what downtown Canton looks like. Clear your head."

"Good idea," Ed replied.

"Great," Tom said, as he turned to go back inside. "See you when you get back."

Ed stepped out of the shade of the building and felt the heat of the sun beating down upon him. He removed his jacket and felt a light breeze begin to cool his body, as well as his temper. He slung his jacket over his shoulder and felt a weight bump into his back.

Why not, he thought.

He discretely reached into the inside pocket of the jacket and removed a silver flask. He shook it and knew that it was still full. He unscrewed the cap, tilted his head back and took a long pull. The Jack Daniels felt good as it burned its way to his stomach. Almost instantly, he felt lightheaded and dizzy.

"Damn, I should have had some lunch," he said out loud, as he started up the street on wobbly legs.

He stopped at a cross street named Tuscarawas. From this position, he had a good look at downtown Canton. Lonely.

Downtown looked lonely. Certainly not like Huston. Cars were coming and going, but they all seemed to be in a hurry to get someplace else. There were plenty of parking spaces on the street. There were people out and about. He didn't need a calculator to add them up, just his two hand and toes gave him the total of all that he could see.

Ed looked to his left and saw a large sand colored building rising high into a cerulean sky. It was topped with golden figures with long trumpets pressed to their lips. *Announcing what?* he wondered. He decided to cross the street and check out the building. In the middle of the street was a small plaza with six benches and four water fountains that were shooting water into the air. One of the benches was occupied by a nice-looking young lady eating lunch from a brown paper bag and reading a paperback.

"Hello," he said as he passed by. She ignored him.

At the building, he read its plaque, "Stark County Courthouse 1893." *Old. This place is old and lonely*, he thought. *I wonder if it were ever a happening place?*

Continuing up the street he passed other buildings that were vacant and on their stones were shadows of names that were once dreams. Further up the street, he saw a huge red sign that seemed to be suspended in midair over the sidewalk. Bold white letters ran the length of the sign that spelled PALACE.

Just before the PALACE, there was a cross street and, on the corner, sat a little bistro. Ed stopped and glanced at the place. It was a modern looking building with two, large cement lions sitting on the sidewalk framing its entrance. A low, wrought-iron fence created an outdoor dining area that contained eight tables. Only one of the tables was occupied and that by a young couple having lunch. They laughed and seemed to be enjoying themselves. Quite a contrast to the young woman he had seen earlier. He watched them for a while wondering how it was that they were having such a late lunch. The woman suddenly glanced up and gave him a friendly smile. Embarrassed, he nodded, smiled back, and quickly stepped inside. The air conditioning chilled him, and it took a moment for his eyes to adjust to the low lighting. There was a small bar with six stools and about ten tables scattered about the rest of the room. He chose the bar and sat on the middle stool.

"What'll be?" the bartender asked.

"A Stella," Ed replied.

When the beer came, Ed filled half of the glass and chugged it down. The coolness of the beer felt good, and he began to feel very relaxed. He did the same with the remainder. He signaled the bartender.

"Another," he said.

"Want a menu?" asked the bartender, as he sat the beer in front of Ed.

"Naw. You got a steak sandwich?"

"Sure do."

"I'll have one. Medium rare. Mushrooms and fries."

"You got it."

Ed was sipping at his second beer when another man came in and sat two stools away. Ed glanced at him. Older, African American. Heavy set. White hair. Maybe, sixties, seventies. The man sighed heavily as he positioned himself on the stool.

"Tough day, Charlie?" the bartender asked as he approached.

"Sure was. That Ms. Johnson in 23B is gonna be the death of me."

"Usual?"

"You bet."

The bartender filled a glass half full of ginger ale, poured in some cherry juice, to add color, and the added a scoop of ice. The man took a sip and smiled contently.

"I ain't a drinker, but George there," he said, pointing at the bartender, "he sure knows how to make a refreshing drink."

"You live around here?" Ed asked.

"Cross the street in them apartments." Charlie gestured with his thumb. "I'm the custodian there as long as Ms. Johnson in 23B don't give me no heart attack."

Ed chuckled. "You from Canton?"

"Born and bred."

Ed's sandwich arrived, and he began to work on it. "Another Stella," he said.

A period of silence ensued while each man ate and drank. A large fly landed on Ed's plate, and he swatted it away with his napkin. After several minutes, Ed turned to Charlie.

"Do you know anything about that place next door called the Palace. Looks like some kind of a theatre."

Charlie's eyes took on a faraway look. It was a full minute before he responded.

"Sure do. Used to work there myself, back in the day."

"What did you do?"

"I was an usher. Only high-class job a guy like me could get at the time. Fifteen I was."

"Oh," Ed responded. He was about to ask another question, but Charlie quickly moved on.

"My grandpap was an usher there too back when the Palace first opened. 1926 it was. He kept a history of the place. Wrote it all down. Gave it to me when he passed."

"How'd it get started?"

"I spect most everbody who growed up in Canton heard 'bout Harry Ink. Local pharmacist that developed a product to treat the sore throat. Tonsiline was its name. Had a giraffe as a trademark. Giraffe. Long neck. Long throat. Get it?" Charlie chuckled.

Ed nodded his understanding.

"Made hisself a ton of money. Mr. Ink died in 1926. Wanted to leave something to people of Canton to express his gratitude. Donated all the money needed to build the place. What you see is what it looked like back in the day. Place has had its ups and downs over the years. Was gonna be torn down at one time, but the people of Canton and some grants had it restored and fixed up to use to this day."

"Quite a tribute," Ed replied.

"Yes, quite a place. Back in the day, all the big names come through here. Big bands, known singers, vaudeville acts. You name it. They all played the PALACE one time or another."

"What about today?" Ed asked.

"Still in use. Movies mostly. Local programs. Some big names. Singers mostly. The management do a good job of keepin' the place goin', and people come and support it."

"I'd like to see it."

"You can. They have tours. I think you can go."

Ed ordered a Jack Daniels and bought Charlie another one of his drinks as they chatted for another twenty minutes.

"Well, I got to go," Ed finally said, as he downed the heel tap of his drink. "Thanks for the conversation."

He stood on shaky legs and nearly fell as he swatted at a fly buzzing about his head.

"You, OK?" Charlie asked with concern in his voice.

"No problem." Ed replied, "Thanks again."

Ed wove his way to the outside where the heat of the day and the alcohol staggered him. He put his hand on one of the lions to steady himself. There was a buzzing close to his ear and a fly zipped past his eyes. He swatted at it, missed, and nearly fell again.

"Damn thing," he slurred.

He didn't remember crossing the street, but he stood under the awning and in the shade of the PALACE. There was a quaint, little ticket booth and an open door to its right. Cool air and the sound of voices came from the opening. Ed stepped inside.

"Hello," a cheery voice said. "Are you part of the tour?"

"Sure," Ed mumbled.

Ed was standing in a large, inner lobby that was dimly lit by candle-like lights that hung from the side walls.

Someone ought to pay the light bill, he thought.

He looked through a glass partition to his right into a large auditorium that had seating for what appeared to be at least a thousand or more people. At the far end of the of the seating was a huge wooden stage that was also dimly lit. Ed began to feel dizzy and a musty smell filled his nose.

"I need to sit down," he said to himself.

At the far end of the lobby above a door, he saw a small lighted sign that read "Gentlemen." He made his way through the small group to the door and stepped into a small lounge that contained seating that was obviously from the past. To his right, another door opened into a restroom. It was decorated with small, bright-colorful tiles on the walls and on the floor. There were several porcelain sinks and urinals along one wall. A buzzing sound filled his ears and a small ache began at the back of head. He turned the handle at one of the sinks and felt the cold water flow onto his hands. He took several handfuls and splashed them on his face. With some paper towels, he returned to the sitting area and sank into one of the chairs. It seemed to embrace him, and he began to feel comfortable and more like himself.

After a while, he rose and stepped back into the lobby. It was vacant.

"Hello!" he called. No answer.

"Left without me," he said to himself.

"Hello!" he called again. This time louder.

His voice seemed to be absorbed by the size of the place, and soon the quiet began to hurt his ears.

"What the hell. Might as well look around myself."

Ed stepped into the main auditorium and started down a lighted aisle toward the stage. He looked up and saw carved statues that were back lit with red lights. He felt that they looked upon him as an intruder. He also noticed the white clouds that were moving across a dark ceiling. Small stars winked at him from their heights. He was inside but felt like he was outside. He stopped at the foot of the stage and looked back at vastness of the place. In the dimness of the theatre, he imagined that every seat in the balcony and the main floor was filled with people. Thousands of eyes were looking at him, waiting for a performance. Was he going to sing? To dance? He could do neither, so he just waved. He could sense their disappointment.

Off to his right, he heard conversation and laughter coming from behind a closed door. He walked to it and saw a sign that read "Dressing Rooms". He opened it, stepped through, and stood at the top of a flight of concrete steps that led below. The laughter and conversation grew louder. As he started down the steps, a buzzing filled his ears and a large fly flew about his head.

"You again!" he shouted and swiped angrily at the pest.

The force of his actions caused him to lose his balance. He reached for the railing but missed. He sensed himself floating through the air, felt and heard a dull thud, then darkness.

36

A distant voiced rattled through his brain, "Are you O.K.?"

He felt drops of water on his face. *Why is it raining?* he wondered.

"Are you one of the acts?" the voice inquired.

Ed forced his heavy eye lids open and looked into a blurry face standing over him. As his vision cleared, the face became sharper. It was strong looking with sharp features that seemed to have a white powder coating. Under its chin was a white towel tucked into the collar of a striped shirt. A pencil thin, black mustache topped the upper lip, and piercing blue eyes looked at him with concern.

"Are you O.K.?" the face asked again.

Ed's vision broadened, and he saw others standing over him all dressed in brightly colored outfits. Costumes was Ed's first thought.

"I think so," Ed replied.

"Here, drink this," a voice said, as he was handed a glass.

Ed tipped the glass back and chugged half of it. He quickly realized that it wasn't water. The liquid burned all the way to his stomach, but he felt instantly alert. He sipped the rest of the glass and attempted to stand on weakened legs. He nearly fell, but the people quickly crowded around him and held him up.

"What's your name?" the face asked.

"Ed. Ed Smith."

"Well, Ed. I'm Banks Kennedy. Are you one of the acts for tonight?"

"Acts?" What do you mean, acts?"

Banks looked puzzled. "Perhaps we should talk in my dressing room." he said. "Come with me."

Ed followed Banks down a long hallway. Many large rooms lined the hall, and each one was labeled "Dressing

Room". Ed glanced into them and saw tables filled with bottles and jars. Bright light bulbs outlined mirrors that were attached to each of the walls. Colorful clothing hung on racks that sat in the middle of each room. In one room Ed saw a calendar hanging on a wall, but what caught his attention was the year displayed on it. 1926.

Odd, he thought, *but authentic.*

The crowd followed Ed and Banks down the hallway and dispersed themselves into the various dressing rooms. Soon the hall was filled the clinking of glass, laughter, and the buzz of conversation. Shortly, someone began to peck a tune on a piano.

At the end of the hall, they came to a small dressing room With Banks Kennedy's name stenciled on the door. Inside Banks sat at a lighted-mirror table, straightened the towel under his chin, and began to apply a light dusting of powder to his face.

"Come. Sit," he motioned to Ed.

Ed entered and sat on a wooden, folding chair. What got his immediate attention again was a calendar. The day, November 22 was circled in red, but the year 1926 jumped out at him.

"Can't be," Ed mumbled.

"What?" Kennedy asked.

"1926. Not possible."

Ed was about to ask another question, but Kennedy cut him off.

"Most assuredly, old chap. It's opening night at the Palace Theatre here in Canton!" Banks said excitedly. "Quite a show. The movie, *Tin Hat* with Conrad Nagel will be shown. The famous dance team of Ruin and Bonita are here. Gel-Mann and his orchestra will play. There are some vaudeville acts, and finally, me. I will be debuting and playing the new Kilgen organ for the very first time. I've come all the way from Gary, Indiana to be part of this. My opening number will be "Valencia". Quite an exciting evening, don't you think?"

Ed was trying to comprehend all of what had just happened, but in his uneasiness, he slowly became aware of the sudden silence that had settled like a blanket on the hallway and in Bank's dressing room.

He looked up and saw a short man and a tall one filling the doorway. They were dressed in grey three-piece suits that were stretched to their limits because of their owner's muscular bulk. Each wore a black, felt fedora with the brims pulled low to cover their eyes.

"Are you Kennedy?" the tall one asked as he pointed at Banks.

"Yes. Who might you be?"

The man ignored the question.

"You know a dame by the name of Victoria Liotta?"

"Yes, we're friends."

"Well, she ain't yer friend anymore."

"What do you mean?" asked Banks incredulously, as he rose from his chair. "Certainly, Victoria can make her own choices about her friends."

"Dats true. But you, yourself, has no choice. You see, Mr. Liotta don't want his daughter hangin' out in speaks with the likes of yer kind."

"Who is this Liotta fellow?" Banks demanded.

"Let's just say dat Mr. Liotta has several business interests here in Canton, and he likes to look out for them and to protect his family from the riff-raff."

"What if I refuse?" Banks asked.

"Certainly, you may choose that option," he replied politely. He paused and stared hard at Banks. "Ever hear of a guy by the name of Don Mellet?" he asked in a quiet voice.

"Sure. He was the newspaper man that was shot and killed several months back. It was in all the papers. So tragic."

"Yeah, we'll go with dat," the short man said with a chuckle.

"Shut up, Angelo! I'll do da talkin'."

The tall man took a step toward Banks.

"Mr. Liotta says if'n you do, you might go the way the way of Mr. Mellett. You, sorta get my drift?" he asked, as he opened his coat to show a black .38 Special in a shoulder holster.

Banks fell back into his chair. Fear etched upon his face.

"We'll go to the police." Ed interjected.

The little guy chuckled again.

"Go head. Just know dat Mr. Liotta and dah chief are pretty tight," the tall one said with a smirk on his face.

The smirk, the attitude, and the audacity of these thugs angered Ed. He sprang from his chair, knocking it to the floor. He picked it up and started to swing it at the two men. The little guy whipped out his pistol and aimed it at Ed. The slug caught Ed at mid-chest and hurled him into the back wall of the room. He slid down it and sat upright as he struggled to breathe. He looked up and saw Banks Kennedy staring at him with a shocked expression on his face. Ed heard a small buzzing sound in his right ear, closed his eyes, and exhaled his last breath.

~

Tom came out of the Grand Hotel, looked at his watch and quickly glanced up and down the street

"Damn," he said aloud, "one hour until the next meeting. Where the hell is Ed?"

He decided to take a jog up the street looking hurriedly into some of the store windows hoping to see Ed. Just as he crossed Third Street, several Canton police cars sped by with screaming sirens and flashing lights. They were soon followed by an equally noisy EMS unit. They all stopped in front of the same building. Out of curiosity, Tom quickened his pace, and by the time he got to the scene, a large crowd had gathered. Several policemen controlled the crowd and kept the building's doors clear. Soon two EMS men wheeled out a body strapped to a gurney. Tom pushed his way forward to have a look. He saw a blue tinted face and a blood- soaked shirt.

"Oh my God!" he shouted.

"You know that guy? A policeman asked.

"Yes. That's Ed Smith. He and I work together. We're staying at the Grand. We were…" his voice trailed off.

"Have to ask you some questions." the officer said.

"Sure," Tom replied absently

The policeman flipped open his notebook and asked his first question.

Tom didn't hear it as he watched the EMS unit speed away and wondered what kind of a story he would have to tell Houston.

ENDNOTES TO EPISODE AT THE PALACE:

When the ambulance gets to the morgue, the attendants find Ed's body missing. A search is underway, but no body is ever found. Ed materializes in Navarre, Ohio with his three other time-travelers in chapter 7's story, Applejack.

Chapter 4: Discovery After the Whirlwind

Written by Mela Saylor

The 8:20 Clock shop in Canal Fulton

1921

First, he was in Norway, then he was here on his hands and knees looking for Jonas's timeflies. Then people came and let them out into the world. And now they were all gone again, supposedly out looking for them, leaving Thomas in the mocking silence of the few hundred clocks that were sitting around the shop.

The silence was deafening. Not one clock ticked, which make his predicament dire. What was Thomas to do?

"Meow." Surprised, Thomas looked down and standing at his feet expecting to be fed, was a small orange tabby.

"Did you come here with those girls?" Thomas bent over and picked her up, thankful for another living being to hold. It wiggled in his arms and he nuzzled the cat's head.

"Hungry, huh?" He stroked the purring cat as he looked around the place for the first time. "I'm hungry, too. Let's go see if there's any food here."

Thomas looked around and noticed a door between two rows of grandfather clocks toward the back and made his way there over the squeaking floorboards. Opening it, he found stairs going to the second floor.

"Wow. I would never have guessed – and thank you, Jonas." Once upstairs, the cat jumped out of his arms and made a beeline to the little kitchen in the corner. Thomas followed and once there in the blue and white kitchen, he started opening cupboards and drawers looking to see where things were.

"Meow." The cat reminded him she was hungry.

"Okay – hold on a sec." Thomas found a few saucers and took one out of the cupboard, turning to look at the cat.

"Now let's see if there's anything in the refrigerator." He opened it and it was empty. There was one overly bright lightbulb on in there. He closed the door in disbelief and turned to the cat.

"Milk? There's no milk – nothing. Not even a loaf of bread." The cat circled his legs purring louder. How could he make the persistent thing understand? He opened the door again to show the cat there was nothing.

"See-?" And sitting there on the top shelf was a glass milk carton and a loaf of bread.

Hey! What's going on?" Thomas closed the door again and thought about it for a moment. "I said milk and bread, and it appeared, so…cheeseburger, french fries and a chocolate milkshake." He held his breath as he opened the door once again and the smell of a cheeseburger and fries assailed him. "Oh wow! Jonas – you're a freaking genius wherever you are!" He retrieved his dinner and poured milk in a saucer for the cat. He addressed the refrigerator again, "ketchup." He sat down at the small table with the cat on the floor underneath and they had their first meal together of many in what would eventually become their home.

Still fascinated with his magic refrigerator, Thomas played with it all afternoon making it produce endless cookies and an array of candy for him and, unfortunately, a live mouse for his little companion. It was a bit of a shock the last time he opened the door and the cold mouse jumped out at him. That's when he called it quits and moved on to explore the rest of upstairs.

On one side of the kitchen was a sitting room painted in blues and greens. One entire wall was filled with a floor-to-ceiling bookcase overflowing with books, magazines and what looked to be instruction manuals. There was a white couch in front of the bookcase with a dark wood coffee table and a rocking chair by the double window at the end of the room. There were several reading lights on end tables scattered around the place and two tall potted plants stood on the floor in front of the windows. Across from the couch and bookcase was a solid green wall with a low console and two abstract oil paintings. The original art was lost on fourteen-year-old Thomas.

On the other side of the kitchen was the bathroom – done in white tile and next to that was a bedroom. There were two windows, one facing north and one facing west. It, like the living room and kitchen, was also done in blues with a single bed, a nightstand with a lamp, a bureau, a desk, and chair. The desk and chair sat underneath the north window, with what appeared to be a radio. The bureau held a selection of clothes in various sizes. Upon seeing all the clothes, Thomas sighed.

"This looks like I may be here awhile, huh?" he addressed the cat who at that point was sitting on the desk looking out the window. She twitched her tail and appeared to talk back to him.

"You have a name? I think the girls were calling you Cora, right? We'll just leave your name alone. I'm sure they'll be back for you. They've got to come back, right?"

There was one last unexplored room upstairs. It was an 8-by-12-foot interior room filled with shelving around the perimeter and a workbench with several overhead lights in the center. Every flat surface in that room was filled with tools and hardware.

"What the heck? Jonas put a junk room in this place? Sheesh!" And with that comment, Thomas slammed the door shut behind him. He didn't open it again for almost 20 years.

Later that night, after he and the cat had both eaten again, he finally meandered his way to the bedroom and sat on the bed. He was still in disbelief, still wired – by everything that had transpired that day, and by the candy he had consumed earlier. He looked at the foot of his bed. The cat had already decided she was sleeping with him and was curled up in a ball.

Thomas got up and opened the window over his desk and sat down, looking out into the night. He could hear the cicadas outside and wondered if those people that he met earlier had found the timeflies yet. How many were there now?

Idly, he started opening the desk drawers, looking inside. The top drawers held pens, paper, and stationery supplies. One of the center drawers held a box of cigars, which he promptly took out and started smoking after locating the matches. He coughed, choked, and wheezed, reacting the way most 14-year-old boys would the first time they are introduced to cigars. Thomas pensively sat there looking out into the night smoking the cigar. When he was finished, he rummaged through the desk again and pulled out one of the blank journals he had earlier found in one of the bottom drawers. Picking up a pen, he began writing.

From the Journal of Thomas Berg

Day 1 – Sometime in 1921?   (I've no idea of the actual date. I suppose I should keep count of how long I'm here, just for the sake of knowing how long I'm here. All I can do is mark the days off on the side of this desk.)

I am worn out. My day began in Norway in the year 1961. I went sightseeing and wound up in an old shop run by what I thought was a kooky old man who in retrospect, really was a wizard. You know, the kind that makes magic. Once there, I was hustled into his back room and then sent hurtling head over tin cup into time and space to where I am now in order to protect this old guy's special insects. I didn't and accidentally broke the vials they were in. Then some nosy people came and let them out of the shop. Now they are out looking to find those timeflies to make things right.

And now I've no idea what day, year, or month it is – but I surmise it is still August since I look out my window and the corn in the cornfield, of which this building I am in is sitting, is over the top of my head.

My name is Thomas Berg and I am 28 years old. I was born in Norway in 1943 and emigrated to the United States as a child with my parents in 1950. We live in Chicago, Illinois, and up until two weeks ago, it was an uneventful life. My father's last brother died and left some property that needed attended to and disposed of, but my father was unable to make the flight because of health problems. So off I went. And here I am. From what I gathered from my visitors today, I am back in the United States. I feel as though I've fallen into a rabbit hole.

I don't know how long I'm going to be here, but I'm very thankful that the old man, Jonas, saw to my basic needs when he sent me here. I don't know what I'm supposed to do now, other than wait. I'm really hoping I wake up in the morning back in my hotel room and that this is all just a nightmare. I need sleep.

Chapter 5: Lamy's
Written by Ron Luikart

Canton, Ohio
2015/1945

Roger stepped out of his office at the corner of Tuscarawas Street and Market Avenue into a driving snowstorm. The wind ripped at his topcoat and tried to pull his hat from his head. The slanting snow beat on his bare cheeks and hands like little needles poking him. The noon weather report had said this was to be the first major storm of the season, and it was shaping up to be one of the worst in the state's history.

Roger was anxious to get to his apartment because it had been a very difficult day for him. He had just gotten fired from a job that he had held for ten years. Plus, soon after lunch his lawyer had called to say that his divorce papers were ready to be signed. Half an hour after the call, his boss summoned him to his office where he was given his notice of termination.

When Roger walked into his boss's office, he had felt like he was going to an execution. Mr. Kelly sat behind his shiny, black desk trying to look busy. Mr. Kelly didn't say anything, just motioned Roger to a nearby chair. After Roger was seated, a movement over his right shoulder caused him to turn. Sitting on a couch near the door he had just entered was his supervisor, Ms. Berringer. A feeling of anger automatically sprang up inside Roger, but it was quickly replaced with fear when he saw an evil smile beginning to form at the corners of her mouth.

He felt that the title of Ms. fit her quite well. She was what he pictured a Ms. to be. Berringer was very plain looking

48

with one of those short haircuts that made her look like a man. She always wore slacks, and more often than not, a shirt and tie. Roger felt that Ms. was a title that implied no identity or personality. It was obvious to Roger that a woman wearing men's clothing was having an identity problem. The other office workers avoided her like the plague and dealt with her only on a professional basis, or when they had to. On the other hand, Roger gloated and enjoyed doing little things that upset her. He never called her Ms. Berringer. It was always Miss Berringer or just plain Berringer. But, now, as he sat in Mr. Kelly's office, he felt that those little pleasures were about to do him in. Surprisingly, a feeling of sadness began to replace the anger and fear that he felt at first. The feelings weren't for himself, but for Berringer. She had been with the company for only seven years, and in that time, she had strong armed and kissed ass to get where she was. She had stepped on and intimidated so many people that very few of colleagues had anything good to say about her. She wasn't a people person. Results were her main goal. Feelings toward people just slowed down what she wanted. Roger wondered if Berringer really enjoyed herself. He suspected not. The sadness must have shown on his face because Berringer's smirking expression changed to a look of puzzlement. She was about to ask a question when Mr. Kelly cleared his throat and began to rustle some papers on his desk.

Roger turned in his seat and faced his boss. He knew what was coming, and his attitude was to let the chips fall where they may.

"How are you Roger?" asked Mr. Kelly.

A stupid question, Roger thought as he suppressed a smile. "Fine, sir," he replied.

"Roger..." Mr. Kelly began and stopped. He rustled more papers. "Roger, I have your job evaluation for the last quarter in front of me, and frankly, it doesn't look good."

Mr. Kelly looked up expecting a defense.

"Yes, sir," was all that Roger could muster.

"As a matter of fact," Mr. Kelly continued, "your performance and productivity over the last several quarters have declined, plus you seem to be very uncooperative."

Mr. Kelly paused. Waited. Roger said nothing.

"Given the difficult economic situation that we're in, I feel now, more than ever, everyone must pull their weight. So, based upon your performance over a period of time and Ms. Berringer's recommendation, I'm afraid we're going to have to let you go. I'm sorry, Roger."

Even though he had been expecting it, Roger felt like he had been kicked in the stomach. His heart began to beat rapidly and sweat formed on his upper lip and in his arm pits. He wanted to say something but couldn't. *How unfair,* was all that he could think. Anger rose in him. He stood slowly, leaned on Mr. Kelly's desk, and glared at him. Mr. Kelly drew back. Eyes wide in surprise. Again, Roger wanted to say something, but nothing came out. He turned abruptly and stormed passed Berringer, who seemed to be trying to hide in a corner of the couch. He slammed Mr. Kelly's door so hard that the whole building seemed to shake.

So, Roger found himself standing outside in the bitter cold. How unfair. He thought he had been doing a good job. Nobody had told him differently, until the meeting. Maybe legal action was the way to go. He soon gave up that idea because he knew he would probably lose that too. It was all so unfair. Right now, he just wanted to get away. The quicker the better. He hadn't even taken time to clean out his desk. Let them do it. He looked up and down the street for a cab or bus, but none appeared.

He left the doorway of the building, crossed Market Avenue and began to walk down Tuscarawas. He paused at the steps of a church and thought about going in but decided against it. He hadn't been in one in so long that going now wouldn't change anything. He continued and the storm descended upon with a vengeance. He was buffeted by the wind. The driven snow blinded him and began to creep down the collar of his overcoat. He pulled it tighter around his neck while his other hand tried to keep his hat from blowing away. After about thirty yards, his feet were soaked from the slush on the sidewalk. His anger grew, and he cursed aloud because he had left his boots back at the office. A delivery truck sped by close to the curb and splashed dirty water on his legs, wetting them from the knees down. He picked up an old beer can and threw it, along with angry words at the disappearing truck. The indifference only added to his frustration. How unfair it all seemed. Melted snow ran down his cheeks and mixed with the tears that had started. He had never felt so helpless and alone. He had tried to pretend that it didn't matter about losing his job and wife. Image had been important to him. Being in control was what he had wanted to maintain at all costs. But, Mr. Kelly, Berringer and the storm had taken their toll. Now, he was exposed and unsure. How unfair it all seemed.

He continued his aimless trek down the sidewalk. Somewhere along his journey, the wind had torn his hat from his head and sent it cartwheeling into the street. He had chased it for a couple of steps, but soon gave up when he saw how futile it was. He was soaked and his hair hung down in his eyes. He let the wind push him in the direction that it wanted.

"Now what?" he said aloud. "What to do?"

After about four blocks, Roger felt completely numb. He just wanted to give up and collapse. Right when he felt that he couldn't take another step, a soft, lavender glow caught his eye during a brief lull in the driving snow. The glow appeared to be about a half a block away. He staggered toward it, and as he got closer, he saw that a sign hanging from a post outside a small structure caused the glow. The sign read, "Lamy's Diner". The structure looked like a railroad car from the 30's or 40's. It had a neat, bright appearance. It sat upon a red brick foundation and had three steps leading from the sidewalk to the entrance. There were four evergreen bushes growing in front of the diner, and a small, white picket fence protected them from the sidewalk. The body of the diner was blue, trimmed in a soft yellow. Large windows ran the length of the diner and wrapped themselves around both ends of it. Soft, white lights on the outside, by each window, gave the diner a warm glow. The roof was a corrugated metal and painted silver. "Lamy's" was written in Old English script on the side of the diner in the same soft yellow that trimmed it. In spite of the storm, the outside of the diner appeared to be shiny and new. He had been up and down this street going to and from work, and this was the first time he had remembered seeing it. Of course, anything could have happened while he was on the bus coming and going. He was usually asleep in the mornings and reading the paper in the evenings. So, he wasn't surprised to see this structure in downtown Canton. The lights inside Lamy's helped to brighten the storm, and they seemed to draw Roger toward the diner.

Roger moved up the steps and opened the door. A sense of warmth and peacefulness washed over him as he stood in the doorway. On his left was a counter and twelve or thirteen stools that ran the length of the diner. They were silver pedestals topped with a red seat. On his right, were seven booths that also went the length of the diner. The booths were next to the windows and looked onto the street that Roger had just come from. They were a dark wood with red seats and sides. Attached to the side of each booth was a pole with coat hooks at the top.

The overhead lights were florescent, but they weren't harsh. The soft lights and the sense of orderliness caused Roger to relax. He felt the tension and anger fall from him like the melted snow from his topcoat. At the far end and behind the counter stood a man. He was busy washing and scrubbing a bunch of carrots and seemed to be unaware of Roger's presence. As Roger stood in the doorway letting the warmth of the diner engulf him, he became aware of music playing. It was a snappy number, and one that Roger was unfamiliar with. The smell of fresh brewed coffee caused Roger's stomach to rumble.

His wet shoes squeaked on the checkered linoleum floor as he walked to one of the stools. He took off his coat, hung it on a hook, and sat at the marble topped counter. The man behind the counter stopped what he was doing and faced Roger.

"Coffee?"

"Sure," replied Roger.

The man moved to a huge, silver urn that was standing at attention along the back wall opposite the counter. He selected a mug from a stack and filled it with the steaming liquid. He placed the heavy, white mug in front of Roger and stepped back. Roger wrapped his fingers around the mug, and the heat began to drive the numbness away. An ache and a tingling sensation started as circulation returned to his hands.

"Cream?"

"Yes, please."

The man went to a small counter refrigerator and took out a tiny porcelain container of cream and placed it beside his cup. Roger added the cream and sipped his coffee. It burned its way down his throat and exploded in his stomach. From there, the heat of the coffee spread through his body like fire through short grass. After a couple of sips, Roger's senses started to return to normal, and he began to feel human again.

"Hungry?" the man asked.

Roger looked up into a pair of deep set, brown eyes. There were little crow's feet at the corner of his eyes that framed them with friendliness. The man appeared to be about thirty years old. *Fairly young*, Roger thought.

"Sure. What do you have?"

The man raised his left arm and gestured to a menu that was located on the wall above the coffee urn. But Roger didn't look at the menu. He was staring at the man's hands or lack of them. In place of his hands, there was a pair of hooks. The man caught Roger looking at the hooks. Roger quickly looked away.

"Hey, don't be embarrassed," the man said. "You get used ta people's looks and questions. It don't bother me none."

"What happened?" Roger asked.

"Lost 'em the war."

"You were in Nam?"

"Nam? Where's that?"

"You know, Viet Nam. Southeast Asia," replied Roger.

"Naw, I was in Italy with Patton."

Roger took another sip of coffee. He was feeling a little confused, but before he could say anything else, the man beat him to it.

"What's yer name? I ain't seen you in here before."

"Roger Davis. What's yours?"

"Ed Lamy."

Roger automatically reached out his hand, but quickly drew it back.

"Sorry," Roger apologized.

"Don't be," Ed said. "I can shake hands, if it don't bother you none."

The hook felt cool in Roger's hand, but there was a sense of warmth that made Roger feel comfortable, and it wasn't caused by the coffee.

"So, what are ya gonna have?"

Roger looked at the menu. He wasn't exactly sure of what he was seeing. The price of a hamburger was 15 cents; coffee, 5 cents; pie, 15 cents, and a sirloin steak dinner was $1.50.

"Are those prices right?"

"Sure. What's wrong with 'em?"

"They're kind of low."

"Yeah, well, maybe I'll bump 'em a dime. You gonna order somethin'?"

"Burger with pickle and ketchup. Coffee."

Ed went about the business of preparing the sandwich and pouring more coffee. While the hamburger was cooking, Ed went to a large juke box that sat majestically in a corner of the diner. It was a Werlutzer that lit up like a rainbow when a coin was dropped into it. He put a coin in its slot and punched some buttons and a lively tune soon filled the diner. Ed jitterbugged with an imaginary partner as he moved back to the grill.

"What's the song?" Roger asked

"Not sure," Ed replied. "It's one of Muggsy Spanier's latest hit."

"Muggsy Spanier?"

"I got all the big names and their latest numbers. Sinatra, Andrew Sisters, Dick Haymes, Kay Keyser, and Glen Miller. They're all here."

Roger sense of confusion came back, and he began to feel a little dizzy.

Ed busied himself behind the counter again, preparing Roger's meal. Little clicking sounds were made as he operated his hooks. After about ten minutes of orchestration, he sat Roger's meal before him.

"Those things don't seem to slow you down any."

"Naw, they ain't so bad once ya get use to 'em. It's all in the shoulder, ya know."

55

Ed slightly moved his right shoulder, and the hook opened. He moved it again, and the hook closed.

"See, purty simple."

"Can I ask you a question?"

"Sure," Ed replied, "and I bet I know what it is. Ya wanna know how I lost my hands. Right?'

Roger shifted uncomfortably on the stool.

"Hey, it's O.K. I don't mind. I'm used to it. People are curious. Yeah, I used to get mad, but I decided, what the hell. These hooks are part of me now. I gotta learn ta live with 'em. Talkin' about it seems to satisfy people's curiosity, and it helps me too. I don't become so self-conscious."

Roger took a bite of his burger and waited for him to continue. Ed's expression changed and a faraway look came into his eyes.

"I was with Patton's Seventh Army, and I was drivin' a Sherman tank. We was a rippin' up through Sicily and Italy, pushin' the Krauts back to Germany. On our way we got into a shootin' match with some Panzers. My tank took a hit that killed my crew. Mangled my hands. They had to amputate. Spent a lotta time in a hospital, but that gave me time to think. I decided I wasn't gonna be no freeloader. So, when I got out of the hospital and got my hooks, I came back here. I always wanted a little business of my own, so here it is. Been four years now."

Four years? thought Roger. *If the war was over in '45, then four years would make it…*

Roger was about to ask a question when the diner door opened. A man came in and sat at the far end of the counter. He was dressed in a tattered and torn, blue denim work coat. He wore a gray snap brim cap that was pulled low over his eyes. From a pocket of his bib overalls, he pulled out a green pack of Lucky Strikes, took out a cigarette, and lit up.

Ed went to the man, and they were soon in a quiet conversation. Ed poured the man a cup of coffee and slid a large slab of pie in front of him. The man gulped the coffee and devoured his pie in an instant. Ed poured a second cup and served a second piece, and they disappeared as quickly as the first ones. After he had finished, the man wiped his mouth on the sleeve of his coat and fumbled in a pocket until he produced a tattered, brown wallet. Ed held up one of his hooks in a gesture that clearly meant "Stop." A heated discussion followed, and at the end of it, the man returned his wallet to his pocket and left the diner.

Ed shuffled back to where Roger was sitting. A look of concern on his face.

"Dave Karnes," he said, in answer to the question Roger was going to ask. "He was with the Marines in the Pacific." Lamy continued. "Came home from the war and found out his wife had been knocked up by some lawyer friend. They run off together. Don't know where. Dave say he'll kill 'em if he ever finds 'em."

"What was the argument about?"

"I wouldn't let him pay for the java and pie."

"How come?"

"He ain't got the money. Been lookin' for work for 'bout a month, now, but he cain't find any, just yet. Dave's a scrapper. He'll land on his feet O.K. In the meantime, I try ta help out. He comes in a couple times a week, and we go through the same routine. I let him come back at night ta clean the place up. Give him five bucks fer doin' it. Dave's proud. Cain't take away a man's pride, ya know."

Roger nodded thoughtfully as he took a sip of his coffee. *Ed's right*, Roger thought, *a man has to feel good about himself.* He looked at the door Karnes had gone through. He was trying to see Karnes again, to see what was inside of him.

"You looked troubled," Ed said softly, as he poured more coffee into Roger's mug.

"Just thinking about what you just said. Pride and all of that."

"Ya have ta have it. Confidence too. How else do ya whip the odds?"

"Yeah, I see what you mean," replied Roger.

"Havin' a tough time of it, Roger?"

Roger told his story from beginning to end. Ed nodded occasionally, but he let Roger talk. This was a listening time.

When he finished, Roger looked up to see Ed studying him closely.

"Life's a bitch ain't it, Roger?"

"Sure is."

"I'm sorry ta hear about yer job and all. You look like a smart fella. I'm sure you'll find something. Have you tried?"

"Not yet."

"Well, listen. Don't let the Kellys and the Berringers of the world get ya down. They're just obstacles and problems to be overcome. I think sometimes it's easy to feel sorry fer ourselves, and when we do that, we give up the struggle. That's when we're beat. Gettin' knocked down ain't where we fail, it's stayin' down that causes the problems." Ed paused. "Did ya like yer job?"

"It was O.K."

"Well, said Ed, "if it was just O.K., maybe ya weren't meant ta be there. Ya have to like what yer doin' and feel good about it."

Ed made a lot of sense. Roger began to feel relieved. *Maybe,* Roger thought, *that's why I screwed around so much. Something to do to relieve the boredom and monotony.*

Ed waved his hooks around him. "This is my world. These hooks give me a lot to worry about, but I gotta go on. Cain't let 'em slow me down."

A sense of understanding began to creep into Roger's mind.

"'member that fella that was just in here, Karnes?"

Roger nodded.

"Well, he's got a load to bear. Soon as he realizes that what's done is done, he'll be O.K. Cain't dwell in the past, and he won't kill nobody neither."

It was finally clear to Roger. Life goes on. The world continues to spin. Man is small and needs to struggle to keep up.

The Werlutzer kicked in another song.

"Moonlight Cocktails. Glen Miller," Ed said automatically.

Roger listened for a while, and then looked up from his plate. Ed was watching him closely.

"Nice place you have here, Ed. Glad I stopped in."

A smile flickered at the corners of Ed's mouth.

"Yeah, so am I," he replied.

Roger sighed deeply and pushed himself away from the counter.

"How much do I owe you?" asked Roger.

"Twenty-five cents should do it."

Roger tossed a dollar on the counter. "Keep the change."

"Thanks."

Roger took his coat from the hook and walked to the door of the diner. The storm was letting up, and it seemed to be brighter outside. He pulled on his coat and buttoned it all the way to the top. He turned and faced Ed.

"See you again," said Roger.

"Maybe," replied Ed.

Roger stepped out of the diner, down the step, and onto the street. The snow and wind had stopped. A city bus roared past and diesel exhaust hung heavily in the air. It halted a block away at a stop. Roger began to jog toward it. Halfway there, he stopped. There was one more question he wanted to ask Ed. So, he turned and went back to the diner, but it wasn't there. In its place was a vacant lot overgrown with weeds and smothered in trash. Roger blinked his eyes hard to be sure he was seeing what he saw. Confusion washed over him. His heart rate jumped about thirty beats. But he remembered his conversation with Ed Lamy. Maybe, he began to think, some things don't have or need an explanation. Where Ed came from didn't matter. It was what he had said and his positive attitude that was important. Courage. Confidence. Determination.

The sun came out and beat warmly across Roger's shoulders as he turned from the empty lot and ran toward the bus. His legs didn't feel heavy, and he felt that he could have run forever.

Chapter 6: Sundown at the Cemetery
Written by Mela Saylor

Canton, Ohio
Late October of 2017

CLANG! CLANG! CLANG! CLANG! In the deepening twilight, the sound of a hammer meeting stone reverberated throughout the cemetery. Violet tipped shadows grew closer as trees darkened in the hazy distance.

Dottie strained her ears, trying to determine where the sound was coming from. From there, when she could figure out where "there" was, she could get her bearings. But the sound echoed off the headstones surrounding her, so she stood still, squinting in the darkness around her. She took a guess as to what direction it was coming from and started walking.

CLANG! CLANG! The sound was getting louder the further she walked south, but the closer she got to it, the more anxious she felt. The air rippled around her and the ends of her short red bob lifted and danced around her head in the static electrical current. From every headstone she passed, she heard phantom voices, some of them calling for her, crying, some all at once, but without any discernable words.

CLANG! CLANG! As she came closer to what she was hearing, she heard a swelling of music in the background on an old radio. Just past the mausoleum on the grounds stood an old woodshed. Its doors stood wide open and she could see a shirtless man with a stone and chisel carving a headstone. His chest and arm muscles rippled as he worked beside the large fire going in the open fire pit. The wood crackled and splintered as the searing flames danced about with the music.

CLANG! CLANG! Dottie felt inexplicably drawn to this man and place beyond her will, drawn to him like a moth to a flame. He was crouched, bent over a head stone by the light of the fire. His coal black hair was down past his ears, a wavy side bang fell over one of his eyes. The voices in Dottie's ears were starting up again, whispering fiercely to her now. She batted her right ear to make them go away, and that's when the stone mason looked up at her. He had aquiline features with a cleft in his pointy chin. His bronze skin was glowing in the firelight and when he looked at her with his light blue eyes, she felt he was seeing right through to her soul. Seeing her, his mouth slowly formed into a deep smile, revealing dazzling white teeth. He tossed his chisel and hammer on the ground and slowly stalked up to Dottie. He smiled down at her.

"Hello there, beautiful." His voice was smooth and low. He was gorgeous in a bad-boy way and Dottie was instantly smitten. She could listen to his voice all night and she blinked rapidly, a slow flush highlighting her already red cheeks.

"H – hi. Um, I'm kind of lost. Could you tell me where I am, exactly?" She had a hard time getting the words out with her voice shaking but she couldn't tear her eyes away from him. He had her mesmerized with his eyes. She could barely remember what she was there for with him looking down at her like that.

The man put down his hammer and slowly walked up to within inches of Dottie, his 6' 2" frame dwarfed her petite 5' 3". He put his hands on his hips and slowly looked her over. He smiled. She could feel his breath on her face when he spoke with his deep voice.

"You, my angel, are within inches away from being the center of my universe."

Dottie looked up at him and saw the fire's flames reflecting in his eyes. She held her breath. *Was he going to kiss her?* She wondered briefly. Butterflies danced in her stomach and the voices came back with a vengeance.

"My name is Vincent." He held out his hand to Dottie and when she gave him hers, he leaned over with his eyes locked on hers and kissed it, burning her hand with his lips. She caught her breath. "Dance with me," he commanded, and Dottie was thrust into his open arms by a force outside herself. Her head spun, and Vincent took her flying around the courtyard with the open fire, their feet barely touching the ground. The music on the radio played on. She closed her eyes to the images waltzing before her eyes – the fire, the moon and the starts overhead. Shadows danced among the fire. His body heat was intoxicating, and she couldn't think straight. After a few minutes, Dottie was able to regain some composure. She opened her eyes. His eyes bore into her as if he was trying to read her thoughts. Yes, this was really happening.

"Vincent," she nervously smiled up at him, still uncomfortably close to this formidable stranger. Attempting light chit-chat, Dottie asked "this music is wonderful – who is the composer?"

"Oh, this is Edvard."

"Who?"

"Edvard Grieg, poor guy."

"Why so?" *And why did Vincent talk as if he knew the composer?* Vincent smiled down at Dottie as he continued to waltz her around by the fire once again. He sighed with a twinkle in his eyes.

"Brilliant man, but a tortured soul. I made sure of that." He grinned wickedly.

"What?" Dottie blinked rapidly, not sure she heard Vincent right. He leaned in closer to her.

"I want to devour you," Vincent whispered, as he exhaled in Dottie's ear, his tongue touched the top of it, sending shivers down her body.

Her eyes flew open hearing his voice purr in her ear. *Was it menacing or seductive?* She couldn't think straight feeling his hot breath in her ear and her heart raced in fear. The voices started screaming at her pleading for her to flee. The two of them were still circling the fire in a frenzy as the full moon crested in the sky overhead.

"No, stop Vincent." When he brought them to a stop, he had her inside the woodshed. The doors slammed closed of their own accord. Vincent held her by the shoulders as he backed her into a wall of haybales. Still holding both her arms, he looked down at Dottie in the semi darkness. She, too frightened to look him in the eyes, looked off to the side. To the right was a newly finished headstone with her name on it. Her eyes widened and she looked at him in terror. Vincent smiled in delight.

"Just tell me what you're looking for and I'll let you go, cara mia." Vincent grabbed Dottie by her chin and forcefully brought her face up to search her eyes. His blue eyes had turned to brimstone red and bore into her soul, scorching her. She caught her breath and trembled in his arms. The music had changed, and tremors were starting in her feet again as he opened his mouth and bent his head down toward her. He sighed, looking her in the eyes.

"You look delicious. I want to feast upon your beauty."

At first, Dottie thought his intent was to kiss her. Instead, his mouth kept opening as if on a hinge. When she looked into that cavern, she saw the pits of hell.

"Nooo." she wailed as her knees buckled under her. Vincent caught her by her throat, his hands going around it in a vise-like grip. And then his hands went right through her neck, holding nothing but the locket she had been wearing. In the twinkling of an eye, Dorothy disappeared completely. The last thing she heard as she was catapulted into time again was Demonico screaming her name.

Chapter 7: A Dance in the Dark

Written by Jean Trent

Meyers Lake Ballroom, Canton, Ohio

January 7th, 1979/1951

Anna Margaret stood staring at the remains of the old ballroom, smoke still spiraling up slowly from the charred timbers on the ground. The wind changed direction and the smoke drifted toward her on the icy January breeze. Her eyes teared up. She was not sure if it was the smoke, the cold, or the huge wave of memory of many nights long ago washing over her that caused this reaction. One night in particular kept coming into her mind. A fly suddenly buzzed by her face, bringing with it a stream of smoke curls.

"What the heck was a fly doing in Canton Ohio in January?" Anna muttered quietly to herself as she watched the firefighters putting out any little hot spots that popped up. A sheen of frost and ice covered their helmets and turnout gear. The firefighters glistened in the dim light of the winter sun. Steam was rising from the ashes, floating through the air, and turning into icicles where it touched the surrounding trees. The combination of the charred rubble and glistening ice everywhere was ironic to say the least.

The building was a total loss. An old wooden structure built in 1924 with years of life pushed through it was easy kindling. Anna was quietly taking in the whole scene. The longer she stood and watched the more the memories swirled on the cold wind. Those memories spun around her with that icy chill filling her head- memories mingled with laughter, tears, and voices of those dead and gone. She was quickly distracted by that damn fly again…

"what in the world"

"how is this even possible on such a cold day?"

"Could the fly have been hibernating in the structure somewhere as it heated up with the flames bringing it out of its winter slumber with cinder and ash?" As the smoke burned her eyes a vivid memory washed over her, taking her back to a cold January night in 1951.

Laughter and chatter danced through the air, twisting, and turning with intermingled notes from the big band that was playing that night. Annie had a lovely red chiffon dress on that fit her slight body to perfection. Her curls framed her face in a delightful way, and she was having a wonderful time. She loved to dance, and the Moonlight Ballroom was the place to be, almost any night, for the mostly younger crowd in Canton, Ohio.

While almost all things were the same there was something different, tonight a faint smell of burnt timber and wires wrapped around the normal aromas. The other odd thing was this loud fly buzzing to and fro almost swaying to the beat. Annie thought to herself, *it is 25 degrees out and there is a fly of all things.* As the fly buzzed by, the smoky odor became more intense-and when the fly would buzz off it seemed to go away. As quickly as it had gone, their minds jumped back to the conversations. The laughter grew louder as the conversation became more boisterous, clearly a direct link to the clinking of ice in glasses. The men were boasting, and the women were giggling. As the night went on, once in a while a slurred argument ensued with bold statements that were silly to those around them. If the boys got a little too loud a very large gentleman in a fine pinstripe suit and hat would quietly escort them out of the ballroom in an almost rhythmic way, his hips swaying to the beat with an arm around each of the culprits not only to escort them from the building but also to support their weight as they stumbled along to his quick pace.

Annie was young, fun, and beautiful; thus she never lacked a dance partner. The men fawned over her like schoolboys - just happy to have a bit of her attention. It wasn't just the men - Annie's bubbly personality and big heart entranced the women also. Mama had taught her through actions, despite a period of hardship she had instilled the gift of a kind heart and sharp sense of humor in her children. Barbara was with her tonight-sisters true to form they could go from a tiff over the bathroom sink to sharing a tube of lipstick. Barbara – the older sister was stunning also, a little slighter, but a big loud sense of humor. Annie looked at Barb and thought this is going to be a night to remember. Just then the darn fly buzzed by again sending seven gentlemen into a tizzy as they swatted at it- creating quite the scene. As it buzzed Annie's face the smell of smoke was so strong it burnt her eyes, she let out a little cough.

"Does anyone else smell that? It smells like something is burning?" With all the hub bub there were murmured "no's" and "I don't smell anything." Annie fumbled through her purse for a handkerchief, as she grabbed for it, she was presented with two from the gentlemen beside her. She politely said, "No thank you," as she gave a little wave of her hankie and dabbed her watering eyes- The fly still buzzing all this time. With all the shooing off went the fly and with it again the pungent aroma disappeared.

As the night flowed along there was dance after dance with the women floating across the floor and the fly occasionally buzzing in and out pulling along behind it a bit of a smoke trail. Every now and then when it popped into view it almost seemed as if an ember fell from the air beside it. Annie thought to herself, *I better slow down on the cocktails, I am seeing things.*

She decided to step outside and get some fresh air; she grabbed her wrap and the arm of a fella and strolled along the lake. Eddie was crazy smitten with Annie and was delighted he was chosen for a little stroll.

The lights glistened off the snow-covered lake. One could imagine the sound of the wooden roller coaster-Comet-clacking along to the beats. The moon reflected off the glaze covering the large wooden monstrosity. The smell of cotton candy and peanuts had been replaced with the cool crisp smell of winter with a bit of pine intermingled, and oddly the faint smell of smoke. The couple continued to walk arm in arm, enjoying being alone while still being aware of other couples embraced in the shadows. The echoes of the ballroom whispered across the lake. Eddie and Annie walked and talked. Eddie was very nervous; despite the cold evening he could feel the sweat running down his side under his sharp deep dark blue suit. His hands were also sweating. Annie was the perfect woman. He knew he never could be able to trick her into marrying such a normal Joe as himself, but he was really enjoying this time walking with her.

Although Annie was young, multiple tragedies had tossed her into the world of adulthood sooner than most. She was very aware of the young men's attractions. She was the baby in the family, but with three older brothers she was educated in the behaviors of young men. Annie knew Eddie was head over heels for her - she would never let on though. She was not ready for marriage, maybe she never would be. That was too much to think about and she was just trying to enjoy the moment.

"Annie," Eddie stuttered, "I sure wish you would be my one and only." Annie hesitated a moment, then with a gleam in her eye she simply said

"Aw, Eddie, you know I can't take a handsome guy like you off the market, I wouldn't have any friends left, my goodness I will be getting glares as it is. I tell you what - when I decide to finally settle down, if none of these beauties has swept you off your feet –I will be yours." Annie could see the glint of disappointment in his eyes –as she was pretending not to notice, in flew that fly again, louder than ever and with an obvious smoke trail dropping embers everywhere.

Eddie exclaimed, "what in the world?"

Annie looked at him "Did you see that fly also? I thought I was going crazy." They looked at the fly, it seemed to hover in front of both of them as if it was trying to say something. Annie was overcome with a strong feeling of déjà vu. Before she even had time to think about it, a ruckus in the ballroom caught their attention and they noticed a brawl by the door.

Annie exclaimed, "Oh Eddie it's Bob - you gotta do something." Eddie jumped into action. The feelings of jealousy, escalated with the warmth of whiskey, had transitioned into physical actions. Bob was a smart guy. He was in love with Barb, but had a little trouble communicating that to her. Annie knew it, Barb knew it, and at times she was a bit ornery with the flirting just to get his goat. Bob's goat had been got and even the cold air wouldn't cool his hot head. Fists were flying. Eddie's job was made easier by one simple fact- the cocktails had affected the hand/eye coordination of the participants of the gallant battle for the love of a woman. Barb was peeking through the window with a grin Annie went to her and scolded her, without any seriousness, and they both laughed.

"When are you just going to give in and marry that boy?" She asked Barbara. They both looked at each other knowingly. They both knew this was probably the best their life would be. Young, beautiful, and able to have fun all while having such a loving mother they both still lived with.

Both girls were very protective of their Mother. Their father had died leaving her heartbroken and the bond with the three of them was unbreakable. Their mother would be up when they got home-didn't matter how late it was. She would make them all a glass of warm milk and ask the girls to tell her about their whole evening, not leaving out the smallest detail. They would fill her in on who wore what dress, who was dancing with who and any other excitement of the evening. It would be a late night tonight with all this excitement to tell her about. They both loved this, and they both knew these were times to cherish. The girl's attention was forced back to the brawl as the fly once again made an appearance swirling around the heads of the contenders- the gentlemen twisting and turning, spinning around and swatting. The more the fly appeared in the evening the thicker the smoke trail behind it. As it buzzed out of the picture what was left was a pretzel of arms and legs to the amusement of all. Eddie was the first on his feet, he held out his hands to the other two-helping them off the ground. After a round of hand shaking and mumbled apologies everyone headed back inside.

It was around this time there was talk of cheeseburgers and fries, and how hungry they all were. Bob was sticking to Barbara like glue. Eddie suggested they could all go in his car. They were thrilled Eddie had the coolest car of anybody. He had purchased a Tucker 48; it was lean and slick a beautiful gunmetal gray color. There were no Tucker's around here, so it was a bit of a phenomenon. Eddie had met Preston Tucker a few years back while traveling for business. While there was a bit of an age difference they had stayed in touch, and when Preston came out with the Tucker 48 Eddie was one of the first in line.

The gang jumped in –the girls careful with their high heels getting into Eddies car. Along with them all buzzed the fly, thick smoke streaming behind it with embers in tow!

Eddie exclaimed "Who's smoking in my car? You know the rules, get out and put it out." They all looked puzzled while swatting and shooing.

"Eddie it is that darn fly again," Annie choked out as the fly buzzed around her head leaving her in a cloud of smoke. There were jumbled rumbles of "What in tarnation," "holy cow!" and "Well I never," coming from the car as everyone frantically tried to evict the fly.

A cold mist burst through the air on the wings of the buzzing fly and snapped Anna Margaret right back to January 7, 1979. As quick as the flashback had begun it had ended with an abrupt halt as the fly disappeared into thin air leaving a brief trail of embers and smoke as the only proof it had been there. Bittersweet thoughts rolled through her head as she headed back to her car. What had happened to that young girl, full of life who loved to dance? *Life*, she thought, *life happened.* Although she was relatively happy her life certainly didn't turn out like that young woman expected it to-but it never really does.... does it?

BACKGOUND INFORMATION FOR APPLEJACK:

After the four materialize together in December of 2016, and not sure how long they will be together or at their current location, they agree to take separate accommodations for the sake of safety so not to arouse concerns about four strangers suddenly appearing. They also agreed to meet periodically and use a history club as their cover. Ed stays in Navarre and Reggie rents a room in downtown Canton. The two women stay together in a rental in North Canton.

CHAPTER 8: APPLEJACK

Written by Edward Klink

Navarre, Ohio, United States

February 2017/August 1901

A group of amateur historians plan a party to celebrate the first law trial of the Canton attorney, William McKinley, former governor of Ohio and president of the United States. Elizabeth Moore is the chief planner and loves the stories about McKinley and how loyal he was to his friends and family.

Edward Smith, from Navarre, Ohio, lives on a farm outside the village and remembers that the J. D. De Fine building was the location of that first law trial. He procures the building for the information symposium, but the only dates open are in February 2017, which is two months from now.

Dorothy Buckley, one of the newest members of the group, loves the different meanings of words that she uses to give deeper meaning to her poems. She says that she will volunteer her artistic talent to make up a flyer for advertising and distribute them to the local schools, coffee houses and libraries.

Reginald Fletcher is to be their speaker because he has written many papers on the assassinations of United States Presidents and in particular, William McKinley. Reginald liked

Navarre because 2016 was the year of the seventeen-year locust and Navarre was infested this year with the red-eyed, six red-legged, cellophane looking winged creature with a single musical note cry which when compounded by another thousand cicadas, was to Reginald's ears, a symphonic sound. The cicadas only live for a single day, mate, and break out of their exoskeleton cases to burrow into the ground and reappear seventeen years later. Their empty exoskeleton cases were all over the ground and bushes at the J. D. De Fine building and drew Reggie's attention.

The preparation is complete, and all the flyers have been distributed. Anticipation is high today right before the event. The four of them, Elizabeth, Dorothy, Ed, and Reggie decide to check the place to see if the tables and chairs are in position, at the invitation of Jack Evans, a local township historian who says he has a surprise for them when they arrive. They see Jack's van parked in front of the De Fine building and park alongside. Reggie is driving and gets out of the car first, followed by Ed on the passenger side as each of them open the rear doors for Elizabeth and Dorothy to disembark. It is a cold clear afternoon as they size up the Matthew House, another name for the De Fine building, just above the Tuscarawas River with the Ohio Erie canal on this near side, running along the river channel. The canal was in continual operation from the 1830's until the big flood of 1913.

The front door opens as the four of them are standing there, looking south at the river and canal which are only seventy-five yards away.

"Hello," says Jack. "You must be the people for the McKinley talk."

Reggie, smiling, extends his hand to Jack for a handshake. "Hi, my name is Reginald, and this is Edward Smith. Ed, Mr.

Jack Evans, and Jack, this is Elizabeth Moore and Dorothy Buckley," as each in turn greet Jack.

Jack holds the door open as the four enter the front conference room.

Jack comes to the front and with a wave of his arm, tells them, "This is where the conference will take place and the restrooms are through that hallway," pointing to the left. "Come over and sit, I have a surprise for you if you imbibe."

Edward and Elizabeth look at each other smiling and say, "We do," as Reggie and Dorothy nod affirmatively.

"There isn't much of this made anymore," says Jack as he reaches under the table to retrieve the bottle of Applejack. "Applejack is a liquor that starts out as hard cider, until a farmer would leave a partial barrel outside to freeze. When it is frozen solid, he would knock the bung out and heat a steel poker in the fireplace as hot as he could get it, then run outside to the hard cider barrel and plunge it through the bung hole, through the ice clear to the center of the barrel, to as pure an alcohol as he could make without distilling. As the poker is withdrawn from the ice, a hole is left, allowing the liquid to pour into a waiting canning jar or two. It has a refreshing taste, but don't drink too much, it's about 100 proof." He sets the mason jar of brown liquid on the table.

They look at the jar. It didn't look very amazing.

Jack says, "There's an old legend that comes with this jar. This is the last jar from an old HUGGEE that worked the canal."

"What's a HUGGEE?" asks Elizabeth.

"A HUGGEE," says Jack, "is the man leading the mules that pull the barges up and down the canal from the towpath, but anyhow this particular HUGGEE gave a taste of his Applejack to a man from Arabia, whose life he had just saved from an attack to rob the barge. The Arabian, in appreciation of his life being saved, put some beans in this jar and told the HUGGEE not to open this jar until he is ready to ride a magic carpet. That old man was my great grandpa," says Jack, "and told this story to my dad, who told it to me."

"What story?" asks Dorothy.

"The story about those beans in this jar," says Jack. "The beans that Arabian put in this jar are from Arabia and will turn into timeflies when this jar is opened."

"What do you mean, timeflies?" asks Reggie.

"Well, according to my dad," says Jack, "this is the bug that carried those magic carpets over in Arabia, but my dad told me that he didn't believe in magic carpets but believed that these insects somehow affected TIME itself. That fits. The rest of the story is that when they escape the jar, just like that Aladdin's Lamp, their buzzing sound is high pitched, high frequency and extremely loud. If they get within ten feet of you, your body will begin to vibrate. You will become dizzy as you vibrate into the TIME continuum for up to twenty-four hours."

"Has anyone ever tried it?" asks Edward.

"You can see," says Jack, "this lid has never been removed."

"Should we try it?" Dorothy asks, thinking to herself, *a mind trip will do me good today.*

Jack asks, "Do you want to try some of this Applejack?"

We are all hesitant at first, but Dorothy jumps up saying, "Yeah, I think yeah, what do you guys think?"

"As long as it's not poison," says Elizabeth.

"Okay," say the other two guys.

Jack gets up and says, "I'll get some glasses." He leaves for another room.

They look back at the glass jar but can only see the light brown liquid. They can't see any beans, but the jar is full, with the thick screw-on lid at the top and the thick greenish glass at the bottom. They don't see any beans.

Reggie says, "Those beans might be pupae. I might know what they are if I can see them." He reaches over for the jar before Jack is back with the glasses.

Reggie holds the jar up to the light but still can see nothing. They stare at that jar, trying to see anything.

"Wait," says Reggie, "I think I see something," They get as close as they can, trying to see. "I'm going to open it," he says. Holding the jar in his left hand against his leg, he twists the jar lid with all his might, but nothing moves. Knowing that the girls will tease him if he can't open it, gives an extra ounce of strength to the twist. The lid moves. He smiles as he sets the jar back on the table and slowly unscrews the lid. There is a little *chirp* as the metal lid slides on the thread grooves in the glass. We all jump at that little sound and then laugh at each other, as Reggie removes the lid. The liquid has an apple fragrance. Our heads touch as we peer into the quart jar. There is something on the surface but before Reggie can reach in to retrieve it, a very high-pitched buzzing sound, touches not only our ears but our bodies as well. The sound intensifies and Reggie is the first to begin to disappear, followed by Edward and Elizabeth.

Dorothy, seeing all three disintegrating, smiles to herself and thinks, *Here I come.*

All four are laying on the floor as their senses return. Reggie is first and notices the other three around him, all holding their ears. They look at each other and realize that the noise is gone, and so is the light in the room. Reggie looks at his watch and notices the time 5:30. He looks outside and sees leaves on the trees. Just moments before there were no leaves and someone turned out the lights. There is a bulb on the wall glowing but not very bright and as he gets closer, it isn't even a light. It's a little fire or is it a candle?

Elizabeth, Edward, and Dorothy now stand up and wonder what happened. The table and Applejack jar is gone and it's dark in the room. They look outside through the front window and door, see the setting sun, and walk outside. The cold is gone, and the trees have leaves on them. Their car is gone and so is the paved road. They look south toward the river and canal and even the bridge over the river isn't there anymore. They look to the north and the B & O railroad tracks are still there.

"We must be dreaming," says Reggie, "Are you guys seeing what I'm seeing or are you ghosts?"

"I don't think I'm a ghost," says Edward, "but I'm not where I was just a few minutes ago."

Elizabeth is next as she exclaims, "Where is our car? Where are all the houses?"

"The noise is gone," says Dorothy, "but where did winter go? This is cool, but do you guys realize that we are not where we were just a minute ago?"

"Can we all have the same dream at the same time?" asks Reggie, as they rally together. Reggie asks that they all hold hands just to make sure none of them is an apparition. As they are holding hands, they hear the sounds of someone down toward the river and see a man shouting at some mules along the towpath, dragging a barge full of goods,
heading east. They run down to him, hoping he is not a dream and will not disappear before they can catch him.

The man sees them coming and shouts, "WHOA" to the mules, stopping the barge. He has never seen anyone dressed like these people and looks questioningly at them as they approach. "Who are you?" he asks.

All speaking at once they say, "We were just at the J. D. Define building for a historical discussion on the assassination of President McKinley, when strange things began to happen.

It was winter and cold, and when we came outside it was warm."

"I don't know nothing about warm and cold," says the man, "or strange things happening to you, but you're right, our president is President McKinley, and I voted for him but he ain't dead!"

"What do you mean, you voted for him?", asks Elizabeth.

"All of Stark county voted for him," says the man, "and you people are all dressed funny. Are you new immigrants?"

"No, we're not immigrants," says Edward.

"Well I thought you might be," says the man, "there's a new group down in Tuscarawas County. They call their town Zoar and they call themselves Zoarites. I ain't never seen one, but I thought you guys might be some of them."

"We must be going crazy," says Reggie as he asks the man, "What's the date today?"

"You must be crazy," says the man, "not knowing the date, it's August 31, 1901, and I have to get back to work, we only got eighty hours to get to Portsmouth down on the Ohio River. Pleased to meet you, but I don't have time to neighbor."

All of them stood there with their mouths open and watch the barge disappear to the east.

"What's the date today?" Reggie asks Elizabeth.

"It's February 19, 2017, or at least it used to be," says Elizabeth.

"He just said it's 1901," says Edward.

"Not just 1901, he said it's August 31, 1901, one day before President McKinley got assassinated," says Dorothy. "Touch me. Am I real?" They touch each other to be sure.

"We're real," they say.

"I'm thirsty," says Elizabeth, "let's go back up to the house and get a drink of water from the refrigerator."

"TIME CONTINUUM," says Reggie.

80

"What?" says Edward.

"Time Continuum is what Jack said about those bugs, the timeflies. If what happened is what I think happened, there won't be any water in the refrigerator because there won't be any refrigerator."

"But I'm thirsty," says Elizabeth. "Oh, there will probably be water," says Reggie, "but it'll be coming from a pump on the back porch, or a bucket in the kitchen."

They walk back to the Matthew House and look north, the way they had just come in their missing car, on a paved road, past many homes, but now there are only two homes on the west side of the street. On their side, there is only a church, on the other side of the railroad tracks. As they get to the front of the only building they are familiar with, they see a man walking toward them from the B & O tracks looking up at the building with a scowl on his face.

Reggie looks hard and says, "I know who that is."

"You mean that guy?" asks Edward.

"Yes," says Reggie, "He's Leon Czolgosc, the guy who killed McKinley." They all turn and look as the man approaches.

"Does McKinley live here?" asks the man.

"No, I don't think so," says Reggie. "Why?"

"I just hate him," says the man, "and I want to spit on him."

"Why do you hate him?" asks Reggie.

"I saw all those little people clapping their hands for him. All he does is steal our money and put people in jail," says the man.

"We need government to build roads and schools and to protect our country," says Reggie.

"We don't need no government, we can protect ourselves," says the man.

"Your name is Leon, isn't it?" asks Reggie. The man can't hear because a freight train is passing at full speed heading west.

"What did you say?" asks the man and comes closer.

"Your name is Leon Czolgosc, from Michigan," says Reggie. A frightened look comes over the man's face. He turns and runs back toward the railroad and moving train. "He's the guy who killed McKinley," says Reggie, "we have to stop him."

Reggie and Edward chase after the man and are closing the distance, not knowing what they are going to do if they actually catch him. The man is faster and jumps on the side ladder of a freight car, but only catches it with one hand and hangs on. As each rail tie rushes past him, he disappears around the curve.

"We almost caught him," says Edward.

"But we didn't," says Reggie. Out of breath, the boys return to the girls.

"Who was that, and why were you guys chasing him?" asks Elizabeth.

"He's the guy who killed McKinley. I remember his picture from the books at the library about presidential assassins. If that guy was right about this date, August 31, 1901, we might have saved the life of the president."

"I'm still thirsty," says Elizabeth, as they all go in the front door. "Everything is so different and there is no refrigerator, but there is a pump on the back porch with a tin cup hanging on it." Each of them gets a drink and all are wondering what to do next. Nothing is believable, everything is unbelievable, where they are, the sights they are seeing and now this guy called Leon. They hear the front door open and look to see who it is.

It's the village constable. He comes directly to them. "Who are you and what are you doing here? We got a report from the house across the street that strangers were breaking into the Matthew House and here I am, but I should be on the other edge of town. Some guy got killed hitching a ride on the 8:20 freight. I'm going to have to put you under arrest for disturbing the peace."

A high-pitched sound that only the four of them can hear begins at the front of the house. The constable's horse also hears it and it frightens him, causing him to rear and whiny in a panic. The constable runs outside of the place to calm his horse.

The high frequency buzzing is coming from inside the house. It quickly envelops the four of them with a vibration that brings their hands to their ears. The Constable sees them through the front door as they begin to disappear one by one. The Constable doesn't believe what he is seeing and knows that he will never tell what he is seeing. "This must be what a daydream is," he mutters as he leads his horse to the north, mounts it and goes to investigate the death of the guy hitching a ride on the freight train.

Consciousness slowly returns to the four and they find themselves at the very same table they left one hundred sixteen years in the future. The jar of Applejack is in the exact same position on the table in front of Reggie, with all of them looking down into the interior of the jar, when they hear Jack return.

"Oh good, you got the lid off the jar, here are the glasses."

From the Journal of Thomas Berg:

Today I had a four-footed visitor in the form of a dog. A black lab, to be precise. Cora and I had been alone here for so long that I had forgotten there was anyone else "out there".

I heard a scratching at the door just before 10 am this morning, and at first, I thought I was hearing things. It took me a full minute to realize where it was coming from. When I opened the door a dog just stood there looking at me expectantly.

"What?" I asked him — and I swear he gave me a big toothy grin. I almost exclaimed "What big teeth you have," but we all know how that tale went!

"You want an invitation to come in?" I guess that was enough for him, because in he came. He just sat there looking around the place. I had the creepiest feeling that dog was scoping the place out. Weird, huh?

Just then Cora came sashaying in from upstairs and her morning nap. It would figure she would take an instant dislike to the dog, arching her back and hissing at him.

The dog barred his teeth at Cora, and I tried to get him out of the place, but he wouldn't budge.

"Out you go, bud," I said to him. And the darn thing answered right back.

"My name is Vinny, got that?"

"Ok – out you go, Vinny." He promptly sat down and glared at me.

Ordinarily, talking dogs would leave me speechless, but in my current world circumstances, (magic refrigerators, invisible housing, time traveling), everything, no matter how bizarre it would have been to me a year ago, seems perfectly normal. I does give me pause for thought, though – how did the dog know we were here?

It seemed like an agreeable, if not nosy, dog – but the minute Cora took one look at Vinny, all hell broke loose.

Fortunately, Reginald appeared not too long after that and I gave Vinny to him to watch for me until the girls come back and get Cora. I'd take a talking dog any day! Imagine the conversations we could have! Anyway, Vinny didn't look very happy when Reginald put a leash on him and disappeared once more. Poor dog

Chapter 9: Mrs. Shymanski
By Caroline Totten

Canton, Ohio
2012

After a private tour, Mrs. Shymanski thought of renting one of the fancy downtown apartments in the old Onesto Hotel that were renovated with fake marble, purring commodes, and bullet-proof glass. The windows offered a view of narrow streets, occasional gunfire, and police chases. This was excitement she could handle from a fifth-floor window.

The inner city of Canton was striving for renaissance and creature sculptures dotted the street corners in rhino postures and peacock colors. Artists opened little shops with a dash of Irish optimism, believing that nobody would steal modern art for not even pawnshops would buy it. Yet the yellow metal chicken on the corner of High Street was bolted down in concrete in case some miscreant assumed scrap metal was valuable and tried to carry off the chicken in the wee hours while the police were busting pot heads and prostitutes gathered in the old houses west of McKinley Avenue between Fifth and Twelfth Streets. This area was occupied mostly by the poor who had been ousted from Cherry Street decrepitude by the extravaganza of urban renewal.

The new federal buildings were supposed to make you think that Roman arches and decorative murals transformed

Cherry Street into high-class safety, but as soon as the sun went down, pedestrians vanished from Cherry and reappeared at Belden Mall in the suburbs, which boasted minimal robberies because clogged traffic prevented escape. Belden Mall was former swampland paved over and made respectable by Dillard's, Macy's, and Chinese buffets that gave discounts to old people who didn't eat much. Mrs. Shymanski didn't eat much, but she enjoyed watching men eat with a fast, rowing motion of the jaw, surmising that males with stuffed bellies did not do stickups. Not that her husby had ever thought of security. He had a kind of innocence that perceived no danger, except in her tart opinions, which he attributed to caffeine. When alive, he made a point to take her to restaurants that served ice cream for it doped her into sleepy and she did not repeat her usual comment. "If the economy is so bad, why are all the restaurants packed with po' folks?"

Most people standing in the long lines and yakking on cell phones wore denim, and in her youth, only the dirt poor wore denim. At seventy, she didn't believe the bullchip that pricey denim was a political statement of equality between the rich and poor. Consequently, she wasn't denim stylish. She dressed in slacks and baggy blouses with long sleeves and high collars, except for funerals and weddings and even then, she did not display flesh. She abhorred scooped necklines, a design promoted as chic regardless of flab, but in other matters, her discrimination ran wild.

Tattoos captivated her. She thought anyone who endured pain to serve as a canvas ought to get a second look because they had seceded from conventional beauty with a flash of primitive drama. She liked primitive art, folk art, fine art, and murals of graffiti painted by teenagers who expressed themselves with a spray can instead of a gun.

Among friends, she waxed lyrical about the Hall of Fame parade, the celebration filled with primal screaming and happy waving, good therapy for fans. Unfortunately, the parade pizzazz dipped somewhat when corporate sponsors cut back and replaced fresh flowers with plastic. But still, she loved it when the inductees into Hall received their gold jackets and cried - former poor boys whose heads were sculpted in bronze and placed on pedestals under the dome where fans gawked in awe at the giants who fought over a ball. Maybe it went deeper than pigskin.

A few days later at the jewelry shop, her old friend, Thomas Berg, said, "Football creates heroes. Scoring with a ball is the civilized version of disposing of your opponent in the name of game."

Thomas was replacing the battery in her TimeNix watch as Mrs. Shymanski looked on.

"What is the uncivilized version?"

Thomas glanced at her with a small smirk. "Gladiators fight for honor and glory to the death. Should a valiant loser receive a thumbs up from the crowd, he gets a hot poker for his fatal wounds."

"Thomas, are you saying that football is a modern version of gladiator games?"

Mrs. Shymanski admitted she had a missing gene that accounted for a certain disinterest in the logistics of battling over a ball, but she watched bug-eyed when men piled atop one another in a kind of sexual play. On the street, such behavior would put you in the slammer.

Thomas shrugged. "I'm just saying. Everywhere the Romans went, the emperor had arenas built. The gladiators represented the power of Rome. Should a slave win the battle, he was granted the freedom to limp through life as a hero."

Thomas Berg seemed a man she could love. He had bulging muscles, nimble fingers and a head loaded with history. Moreover, he listened to her opinions with a patient tolerance. "I suppose football is necessary to the economy and not nearly as goofy as Pet Spas," she said. Warm baths, nail clips, carpeting and TV were the pet indulgence of country club patrons, who sipped cocktails and swooned over the details like superior lovers of the canine kingdom.

Mrs. Shymanski no longer had a poodle that dragged her around on a leash and did its business in public, which was as acceptable as rowdies littering with cola cups and half-eaten burgers. After a while she replaced scooping doo with a dog fence round the yard, a useless expense because Prince, the poodle, became doggy dysfunctional and promptly died. This loss simplified her lifestyle, and she could now think about an apartment. She had to - because the yardmen wore dark glasses and looked into the windows, and she had the feeling that lust for her jewelry could get messy.

She and husby had lived in an apartment shortly after the wedding, and the horror of thin walls, the sound of creaking beds and whispers, rushed them to buy a tacky row house, but when they learned the previous owner hanged himself in the basement, they promptly moved to a dwelling with a yard like a park and neighbors who practiced privacy with religious devotion. Consequently, the thought of returning to an apartment carried a shade of resignation for maintaining a house was troublesome without husby. He trusted plumbers, electricians, and TV repairmen as if all males were comrades, a perception not shared by Mrs. S, who, having been accosted by suggestive names like honey and sweetheart, did not want to be alone with a stalker.

Nor was she certain that Thomas Berg would make a good second husband. From dining with him on occasion, she had evidence that his favorite food was hot salsa. She thought habanera peppers were poison that kept you chained to the commode. Habaneras interfered with independence. She prized independence and a fifth-floor apartment offered it. Even if she had to haul ass to Belden Mall to buy organic, she could ride the motorized cart through the market and pick up a little sustenance to disrupt the restaurant routine. She wasn't sick, feeble or toothless yet. She could knit, watch TV, read, and socialize for several hours without yawning and showing her gold-filled molars. Her gold molars were the work of a charming dentist who said that gold would last for-evah. Forty years with the same dentist and he did the unthinkable. He died suddenly, and she could not warm to his replacement for he looked twelve years old and was a plaque fanatic. She felt like a victim of overzealous plaque control and decided to take her plaque with her to eternal life. Not that she believed that she would be beamed up into the eternal cosmos like a tourist with a passport.

At her age, one aspirin knocked her out for days, and five would certainly dispatch her to oblivion should she become sick and tired, but on Sundays when Thomas Berg came to visit, she was glad to see him. Usually, he toted a bottle of wine under his arm. He was a good man and quite tolerant of her opinions. He had plenty of own and alerted her to the latest computer scam or worthy horror movie.

Sometimes she asked, "How do you know this stuff?"

He replied, "I get around."

That was the only conversation that pertained to his travels. He seldom spoke of trains, planes, or ships, except to remark, "I will outlive those contraptions."

Her most depressing fear even in daylight was that Thomas wouldn't outlive the tulips. When he coughed, she quickly served hot tea with honey and kissed him in the middle of the forehead with friendly humility. He was important to her existence even if she had to wear a girdle to hold up her spine. Somewhere out there, the cosmos would have to wait. She couldn't shirk the duty of a friend simply because being wrapped in a cloth and laid to rest was easier.

She thought disintegrating naturally in a pine box in a wilderness cemetery was more environmentally friendly than an egotistical copper boat that took eons to dissolve to dust, if it ever did. Thomas, on the other hand, never worried about eons. He liked a daily shot of whiskey with sugar cubes and a snack of caviar and crackers. Because he understood high maintenance, she asked his advice. "Do you think I should move to an apartment in the renovated Onesto Hotel?"

Without hesitating a moment, he said, "Stay in your house." He went so far as to suggest that her suspicion of the yard crew was unfounded; the window peeping was merely the curiosity of workers bored by grass.

"Yes, that's one way of looking at it."

She considered that possibility, but drew the line when Thomas suggested that she adopt his big, black Labrador for security. His dog was so friendly, it wouldn't protect anything, but its food bowl.

Consequently, she closed the drapes whenever the lawn crew was afoot. The crux of the matter was she had dismantled the house security system because the alarm terrified her, not to mention practically blowing out her eardrums. She wouldn't wish that sort of punishment even on a thief. Instead, she resorted to a window sign: Neighborhood Watch. It implied camera and police surveillance.

She supposed the sign frightened solicitors to the straight and narrow even though the best people often slipped and muddied themselves on that path. She didn't tell Thomas about the dismantled alarm for fear he would install his Labrador in her house and that mutt had a habit of slobbering on the furniture.

Now at night, the glaring outdoor lights announced to the whole world that she was alone, but she kept a can of pepper spray beside her bed in case somebody picked the double locks. Being caught in her nightgown with her hair down canceled the notion that scarecrow seventy was the new fifty. The genius who devised that hoopla was selling statins, pills that pushed cholesterol down and profits up. She knew it from experience.

Occasionally, she endured tests on her vitals. The hunt for cholesterol, sugar and other aberrations inflicted procedures that resulted in an arm swollen for two weeks from a sadistic needle. She wasn't anti-medicine but preferred to make her own.

In the herb garden she had a comfrey plant and she soaked the leaves in witch hazel, Vodka, and rice vinegar with sprigs of mint and rosemary. After filtering through cheesecloth, the consistency was like sun tea, and she sprayed it on her feet before and after serious walking. She shared it with friends who thought it was a miracle drug for aches and pains, but Thomas Berg didn't use it because he couldn't drink it.

"Skin is the largest organ of your body," she said as if Thomas didn't know it. "Comfrey spray won't ruin your liver." This implied that she did not approve when Thomas drank whiskey, watched horror movies, and fell asleep on the sofa with his dog, an affectionate beast that attracted flies.

Without apartment approval from Thomas, she rambled around her house, sat by the window with her morning coffee and watched the baby squirrels do gymnastics on the bird feeder. The old squirrels had vanished, and she supposed they were recycled in the hawk's belly or by maggots. But she didn't dwell on maggots for she was busy, checking out computer scams that were more interesting than knitting slippers. There was always a new banking scam to discuss with Thomas although his bank was a coffee can.

Nobody could write checks on deposits in a coffee can. Thomas anticipated the day when a timefly virus would shut down J.P. Morgan, but Mrs. Shymanski was much more trusting. "It could never happen," she said.

Thomas didn't argue. He merely offered some financial advice. "Put your money in a coffee can."

Mrs. Shymanski sighed and ignored the remark. Thomas was her hugging station, not her banker.

She rose from her chair, collected a few McIntosh apples from the bowl, and tossed them out the door. The squirrels liked a tart treat, and she had visions of a seed being recycled into a tree. That happy thought followed her to the kitchen where she rinsed the coffee stain from the cup. For a moment, she gazed at the cup. She used it daily, but it wasn't chipped. The blue inscription on the mug was her name - Gloria Livia Shymanski, a mouthful, not a tidbit, and she chuckled at the thought of her favorite mug as a curio at a garage sale - someday.

Someday? She was quite surprised and dismayed when she found a note stuck to her front door.

I'm off to the gladiator games on the moon. Take care of the battery in your watch. Time flies.

It was signed. "Your time-share friend, Thomas."

Chapter 10: Charles S. Price
Written by Ron Luikart

Lake Erie

2013/1913

Just after crossing the Peace Bridge at Buffalo, New York and heading north twenty miles into Canada on the Queen Elizabeth Highway, there is an exit for a small town named Thorold. That's where David was going. It had been an eight-hour drive for him to get there, but when he had left for work that morning, he had never had it in his mind to go to Thorold. However, when he came to the traffic light just before the interstate that would take him south to his job, a little voice said, *don't go*. So, he turned north.

2013 had been a tough year for him. His divorce was finalized, and his company was being downsized. The boss had called David into his office several days earlier and gave him the news.

"Cost cutting…. Shifting sales focus…. Possibly relocating company…. No reflection on your abilities…. Six months' notice…. Appreciate your work…. Glad to give you a recommendation…. Good luck."

The news staggered David. After twenty-three years of busting his ass and making sacrifices that involved his family, and this was what it all meant. Nothing. But what really knocked him to his knees was the meeting with his doctor the next day. The tests were all back, and there was nothing that could be done. The cancer was inoperable. Two stinking words.

"Six months."

The words bounced around in his head like a series of echoes. He began to scream and pound the steering wheel as he drove. Some people who were trying to pass him noticed his behavior and looked in his direction,

"What the hell you lookin' at?" He had shouted and sped up to distance himself from them.

Somewhere on the QEW, fatigue finally caught up to him, so he pulled his car to the berm, stopped beneath an overpass, and got out. The breeze had picked up, and he began to feel chilled as he stood in the shadow of the overpass, so he walked a few feet and into the sunlight. He closed his eyes and took a deep breath. When he opened them, he saw a small bird struggling against the wind. It had a piece of straw in its beak. He watched the bird and silently cheered it on. Finally, it reached one of the crossbeams where it had a nest. The straw was placed in the nest and arranged just so. After the chore, the bird rested and glanced at him. He wondered if the bird had a feeling of accomplishment in its breast. He took several steps toward the bird, but his movement startled it, and it flew away.

Maybe the last days won't be so bad, he thought. He got back into his car and drove on.

He exited at Thorold and followed the familiar streets because he and his family had been here many times for relaxing weekends. He drove down the shaded streets until he came to "their" place. The Lock Seven Motel was a white three-story building that had twenty-four rooms and was surrounded by large oak trees and a well-kept lawn. He parked and went into its small lobby. A young girl was dancing to music that he could hear from the headphones that she was wearing. He rapped loudly on the counter.

"Yeah," the girl said as she turned toward David.

"I'd like a room."

"Sure. We got plenty this time of year. Any particular one?"

"Anything on the third floor will be fine."

"How 'bout twenty-two? How long ya' stayin'? "

"Couple days. Twenty-two is fine."

David took his key and went to his room. It dawned upon him that he didn't have any luggage, and it felt strange. With his family, he was always carrying something, but now it was different.

Room twenty-two was a typical motel room. Two beds, a chest of drawers, TV, two chairs, and a small desk. The bathroom was small with thin, white towels that had a slight smell of bleach about them. He walked across the room and out onto a small balcony. This was what he enjoyed most about the motel. Less than the length of a football field from where he stood was Lock Seven. The lock was part of the Welland Canal that was used to lift and pass all of the Great Lake ore boats and Atlantic ships around Niagara Falls and into the heartland of America. He had often daydreamed about the ships and all of the great adventures that he was missing. He had decided at one time that if he ever got the chance, he would get on one of those ships and see where it would take him. There had been some opportunities for him to break out of his routine, but he never did. There was always work, a kid's game to attend, or something else. Now, as he thought back on those missed chances, he began to realize that maybe it was fear that had stopped him. Fear of doing something different, or the fear of drawing attention to himself, or the fear of appearing to be selfish. Whatever the reason, the opportunities had come and gone, and he had stayed behind in his hum-drum life.

He remembered that he would keep a log of the ships that passed through Lock Seven when he was visiting with his family. After the weekends, he would look back through the log and wonder where each ship came from and where it went after it passed through the lock. He went back into his room and took a pad of paper from the desk and settled himself at the window to begin a new log. He didn't have to wait long for ships to appear. He noted their names, homeport, company name, and the type of ship that it was. He was occupied for several hours and soon had a list of eight ships. He was fascinated by the lock operations, the men moving on the ships, and just dreaming.

After a while nature called, so he took a break. When he returned, he saw another ship approaching the lock, but it was different from the others that had passed. It looked older and not as well kept. The wheelhouse was smaller, and the stack was taller and not as rakish. Black coal smoke poured from the stack as opposed to the diesel exhaust from previous ships. He could just make out its name on the bow, *Charles S. Price.* He scribbled the name into his log. As the ship got closer, he had a strong urge to be near it, so he left his room and ran down the street that led to the edge of the lock. When he arrived the *Price* was just beginning to nose into the lock. The edge of the lock was so close to the ship that he could reach out and touch its side as it slid passed. The ship smelled of age and mildew, and its side was streaked with rust and spotted with patches of red lead primer. As the ship moved into the lock, David reached out and touched it. The side was rough, and a freezing chill radiated up his arm and through his body. He felt cold, and fear caused him to turn and run away. Before he had gone far, a shrill whistle stopped him, and he turned to look back at the ship. He saw the dark figure of a man standing at the back of the ship motioning with his arm for David to return.

"What!" David shouted.

The man didn't respond, but he kept gesturing for
David to come back. David retraced his steps until he
stood just below the man. A rope ladder dropped from the
deck, and without any hesitation, he climbed it. When he stood
on the deck, he noticed that it was covered with rotting
seaweed and a thin coating of gray mud. He looked for the
man, but he was gone. He had turned back to the ladder when
another shrill whistle drew his attention to the forward part of
the ship. There was the same man motioning for him to come.
He turned and walked toward the wheelhouse.

When David didn't check out at the proper time, the
owner became concerned and went to his room. When she
knocked, there was no answer. She unlocked the door and went
in. Nothing missing, except the occupant. Something wasn't
right, so she called the police.

During the investigation, one of the officers noticed
David's log.

"Look at this."

"What about it?" "

"Looks like he was keeping a list of ships."

"Yeah, he was. But look at this last entry."

"Charles S. Price." So?"

"There was a small article in this morning's paper about
the *Price.* Some kind of an anniversary. Seems she disappeared
with all hands during a storm on Lake Erie in 1913."

Chapter 11: Time Amok
Written by Mela Saylor

Jackson Township. Ohio
2027

Dottie didn't quite land on her feet this time and found herself tripping over a few misplaced paving stones. Now that she was keenly aware of the potential danger to her mission, she held still for the longest time and listened for any signs of life in the cemetery. She heard nothing but the cold wind rustling the trees like an animal in wait.

Something was wrong. She could feel it in her bones. Her first clue was the discordant cacophony of the insect noises – no consistency or rhythm to what she was hearing. She brushed the dirt off her skirt and looked around. It was sundown and there was just enough time to find Thomas. Honking geese flew overhead, she looked up and did a doubletake, squinting into the setting sun.

"What the heck? That can't be right."

The geese were not flying in formation: they were scattered everywhere and flying at breakneck speed toward safety. Dottie looked around. It was the same cemetery as before, but now everything had changed. Something had happened. But what? Needing to find Thomas she followed the geese, away from the coming darkness, not taking any chances. Noticing the newer head stones on her way out of the cemetery, she crouched to take a look at the dates. They read 2027. This big jump ahead in time made her uncomfortable and hoping she could still find Thomas before it got any later.

Newer headstones soon became farther apart, and she now found herself walking up an embankment where there were none. The sun had set as she crested the top of the small hill, but there were lights reflecting off the clouds ahead. She soon saw a smattering of lights down below what should have been a cornfield. Where there should have been a farm, Dottie saw many styles of rusted cars scattered all over a paved five-lane road, including buildings on the south side, some of which were lit. She could hear the electricity sputtering in a few downed wires twisting like live snakes in the wind. Dottie made a mental note to steer clear of them.

As she cautiously walked down the hill toward this strange area, thunderheads gathered in the sky. A few higher clouds periodically lit up with dry lightning. She jumped when the thunder boomed.

Where was everyone? Is this where Thomas's shop was now? How was she going to find it? The questions circled in her head as her stomach clenched in anxiety.

Dottie started walking into the wind. The first thing she noticed was that the entire place appeared to be abandoned. A few lit and sputtering marquees were still working in places. One that caught her eye was beside a clock tower. The hands on the clock were spinning backward, and the marquee read "The time is now – the time is now – the time is…".

As the wind became stronger, she heard Vincent laughing at her in the wind as it whipped down the road.

Then she heard it, the sound of a motor getting louder. She looked at the watch Thomas had given her. It was spinning out of control.

"This can't be good."

~

Dottie stood rooted to the spot in the middle of the road. She was exhausted, hungry and in need of a bath. She was also worried and angry with everything she had been through by now.

The thing coming toward her in the darkness sounded like thousands of angry bees and the sound got louder the closer it came.

"If this thing I'm hearing is Vincent coming after me, I'm DONE – he can just have me," she yelled, fuming.

And that's how Guy found her – in the middle of the road, hair and skirt blowing in the increasing wind, eyes blazing, and arms crossed in front of her.

The motorcycle stopped in front of her. The man cut the engine and the sound of the wind resumed. He rolled his bike right up to her and she didn't flinch. The burly man with the once brown but now greying facial hair removed his helmet and looked at her.

"Are you crazy, lady?"

Dottie blinked rapidly, trying desperately not to cry, her arms crossed in front of her and trembling.

"They don't call me Dottie for nothing." She gritted her teeth. As she glared at this stranger, a few tears escaped and ran down her face. In her stubbornness she refused to wipe them away.

"Hey there – I'm sorry. Are you okay?" The man got off his motorcycle, put up its kickstand, and looked around before he spoke to her again, this time lowering his voice.

"Is your name Dorothy?"

Dottie gasped and took a step backward.

"Yes," It was more of a question. "who are you?"

"My name is Guy Davison, a friend of Thomas's."

"You are? That's fantastic! Where is he?"

"I uh, he's not here." Guy shifted his weight and stuffed his hands in his pocket. He looked away.

"Can you take me to him?" She eyed his bike, wondered what it would be like to ride one of those things.

"Sure, but before I do that – take a look around you."

Dottie looked around briefly, not sure what Guy was trying to point out, but she knew she didn't like the place. The wind howled down the road. She thought she heard laughter.

"Where is everyone?"

"Whoever is left is in hiding because all hell has broken loose."

"So... what happened?"

Guy sighed and took hold of Dorothy's arm.

"Let's get out of here – we're too exposed – and I'll explain further."

Riding with him on the back of his motorcycle was like riding with the wind. She closed her eyes and held on tight. When the engine stopped, they were back at the cemetery. Guy led her to a memorial bench, and they sat down in the dark, their only illumination the reflected light in the clouds that came from the Belden area. He cleared his throat.

"Let me see if I can explain this right. There was a 'bug' in the electrical grid. A real bug, probably more because of the massive failure of the system and everything electrical, motorized and mechanical went haywire."

"But your motorcycle is working."

"Just barely – I have to Geri-rig the damned thing. Sometimes things work, sometimes they don't. It just depends if the gods are on your side that day." Guy gave a small laugh in the dark. He took a cigarette out of his pocket and lit it. After a few moments he continued.

"Things are backwards – and no one really knows what time it is anymore, so everything has broken down." As they sat in the dark, a mother goose walked by followed by her goslings. They were walking backwards. Guy looked at Dottie staring at what was now a common occurrence and smiled.

"Yeah – it's that bad."

"You said you'd take me to Thomas."

"I did," Guy pointed to the headstone beside them.

"No!" Dottie went over to it and fell to the ground. Guy took out his flashlight. The headstone read:

Thomas C. Berg
1934 – 2023
He ran out of Time.

Dottie started crying, all her pent-up emotions spilling out of her.

"I'm too late! I'm too late…"

Guy picked up a hysterical and sobbing Dottie and gently shook her.

"Snap out of it! You still have time to fix this mess. Go back – find Thomas in 2020 while he's still lucid – and go back and take care of those damned flies." He moved her out of her eyes,

Dottie drew a ragged breath as she wiped away tears. "Okay."

The last admonition she heard from Guy before she disappeared again was his yelling an admonition at her as she faded away. "And stay away from Demonico!"

Chapter 12: Taken Out

Written by William Alford

Jackson Township

2018

To say my niece was spoiled would be an understatement. Looking back, she seemed like a caricature, something out of a dreadful pulp fiction novel. Of course her hovering parents and my doting mother and father didn't help.

"Well, she is our *only* grandchild," my mother used to say; her voice always accusatory in tone.

Denise and I decided from the outset to be childless. I had no patience for children. I knew I would kill them eventually if I had any. Plus, the thought of introducing a child into the world given its current state was almost a crime in itself. So I endured the criticism at every family gathering, until my wife reached the age where having children was no longer feasible.

Abby continued to blossom into a rose who was anything but delicate. Despite her angelic face, thorns described her best. And she continued to be showered with affection, receiving all she asked for. Breast implants at fourteen, a slight crook in her nose corrected, Lottie's Salon awaited her arrival every Friday at four. At the end of each season, she tossed all her clothes into the trash. Wearing the same ensemble for more than three months was unthinkable for Abby.

She began dating at fifteen. Her beaus had to meet a list of requirements more rigorous than working for the CIA.

Handsome, from a prestigious family, intelligent, curious, and slightly naive. All had to attend a private school, like herself.

Tommy Crookshanks fit all the requirements. His father managed the First Federal Bank downtown, while his mother steered most of the city's charitable events. Tommy's future appeared promising, already having been accepted to Yale. That all would change on a cool September evening.

Abby burst through the front door of her home, crying uncontrollably. Her Gucci Jersey dress hung off one shoulder and ripped up the center. The young woman's makeup was smeared; she looked like a sideshow attraction. She collapsed in the foyer and whimpered, "He raped me, Tommy Crookshanks raped me."

Her parents surrounded their daughter as if danger lurked only inches away. She explained in detail how her innocent date with Tommy had gone horribly wrong. The young man parked his father's Lexus in a deserted lot; he dragged Abby into the car's back seat and forced himself on her. Abby bolted from the vehicle, threw off her high heels and ran the three miles to the house. She pointed to her bloodied feet.

Abby convinced her parents not to call the police or press charges. Tommy's family settled to avoid public embarrassment. A month later, the elder Crookshanks presented a check made payable to Abby for a $100,000. Over the following year, fragments of the scandal drifted around social circles. The Crookshanks reluctantly moved as they faced growing resentment. Tommy never attended Yale, five years later his body was found floating in the New Florence River.

When she turned eighteen, I wrote an essay for Abby that got her accepted into Cornell. Pure fiction, but one of my better efforts I must admit. My hopes that college life would set her on a better course would not happen.

Never an outstanding student, she excelled in college; I chose not to enquire how. After graduating from Cornell with honors, she landed a job with a prominent real estate development firm in New York. Within a year, the company's VP of Marketing had divorced his wife and married Abby. He was twenty-four years her senior.

The marriage lasted nine months, the divorce granted Abby two million dollars and $5,000 a month for life. The pattern was set; two more jobs, two more failed marriages, two more exorbitant payouts from ex-husbands.

I last saw her a year ago. She drove her Bentley up my driveway, two wheels onto the grass. I'm sure she did it intentionally. Abby and Denise never got along, I'm glad my wife was still at work at Starbucks.

Abby slid into a well-worn wingback chair. "I'd love a Chablis."

"I have some Carlo Rossi from Walmart. I'm short on funds... I don't have the income from three ex-spouses."

My comment had no effect on Abby, she only smiled. "I'll take it, I need a drink."

I placed the bottle and a glass on the side table. She filled the glass and downed its contents.

I studied her. She was almost twenty-eight but looked years younger. *Not fair* I thought. "Father died last summer. I thought you'd at least make an appearance. He did take out a second mortgage to help support your lifestyle and education."

"I was in Montreal, couldn't get away." Another gulp of alcohol rolled down her throat.

The wine relaxed her, she opened up. She talked of her exes, their weaknesses and stupidity. She talked of investments and then revealed the main source of her wealth – at least alluded to it.

"Oh, just information here and there– *on the fly*." she giggled at her private joke, then hiccupped. The topic then shifted to Tommy Crookshanks. Abby revealed how she seduced the unsuspecting young man, shredded her own dress, and faked the entire incident. All deliberately calculated, right down to her bloody feet. She smirked at her cleverness. "Too bad he died. That surprised me. My second husband shot himself... I lost money on that one."

At that point I was ready to shoot Abby myself; it would be a service to humanity I thought. But spending even one minute in prison, the woman wasn't worth it. "I think you better go Abby... now." My jaw tightened.

She grabbed the bottle and got into the car. The Bentley cut across the lawn; severed turf flew into the air.

The next day, my brief encounter with Abby still left a bad taste in my mouth. A taste I had to wash away. I walked to the nearest watering hole, a mile from the house. I planned on getting drunk; I didn't trust myself driving home. The parking lot was empty except for two cars, probably the owner and bartender I surmised.

I pushed through the door; the room was cool and dark. Just what I needed, the perfect place to get lost, a corner of the world with no zip code, where no one could find you. There were at least a dozen people scattered about, all sitting by themselves.

I positioned myself on a barstool that felt slightly sticky. A barmaid who could have passed for a wrestler approached. She stared at me but said nothing. I wasn't a drinker, I thought back to my college days. I blurted out the only drink I could remember. "Rusty Nail, please." She nodded, within twenty seconds, she set a small glass in front of me.

It went like that for nearly two hours, drink after drink. I stared at a revolving Budweiser sign that suddenly morphed into something beautiful for me. Despite the lack of conversation, the bar still seemed busy. The clink as the barmaid washed the glasses, the hum from the machines, and the endless drone of country music that all sounded the same. Everyone kept to themselves, but I felt eyes studying me.

I looked around the room. Each patron gazed into their respective glass of poison, except for a man sitting in a corner booth. His eyes were transfixed on me; he raised a can of Pepsi and nodded. I turned my head back towards the Budweiser sign.

A minute later the man slid onto the stool beside me. "Want to talk about it?"

"Excuse me," I replied.

"All the drinks in the world won't change your situation. When you walk out of this place, everything will still be the same. Except, you'll have a hangover. I might be able to help."

I refused to even look at the man. "Help someone else in here mister. And stop the Ronald Reagan impersonation."

"Oh, I know everyone in here. I can't help them. My name is Vincent – I don't use my last name. It's always easier talking to a stranger, someone with no skin in the game. I guarantee one thing, after today, you'll never see me again. Come on, get it off your chest, tell me everything you know about Abby. I promise you'll feel better. And it's not an impersonation, this is my real voice."

To this day, I don't why, but I told the man everything about Abby, who she knew and the last place I knew her to be. And despite the stranger's reassurance, I didn't feel any better.

The man leaned back on his stool. "I've encountered worse, not many mind you, but worse." He reached into his suit jacket and placed a business card next to my glass.

I picked it up and studied it. It displayed only three words, Take Out, Inc. No phone number, email, or business address. "What's this?"

"I represent a firm that makes problems go away."

108

"I don't understand."

"Well, let me spell it out for you. Abby is a problem; my firm can make her go away. That's really all you need to know."

I dropped the card onto the bar. "This is a joke, right?"

The stranger retained his deadpan expression. "I don't deal in humor."

"Okay, okay. Let's just say, I agreed to… make this problem go away. How is that going to happen? And how much is it going to cost me?"

"How it happens varies, you don't have to worry about that. The firm is supported by numerous benefactors who wish, for obvious reasons, to remain anonymous. There is no cost to you. All you have to do is place an 'X' on the back of that card. The rest will be handled. Easy peasey is the best way to describe it."

"What the heck." I scratched an 'X' with a gold-plated pen provided by the stranger. I pushed the card towards him. "That's it, don't you need more information?"

"You've provided enough facts to set the process in motion. My firm possesses the resources to take things from here. Thank you, I don't shake hands." The man saluted and left the establishment.

The barmaid approached and leaned into me. "I think you've had enough. When my customers start talking to themselves, it's time to leave. That'll be thirty-five.

I shook my head, tossed her two twenties and left. I really *did* have too much to drink I thought.

My life continued as usual until a story caught my eye on the evening news two months later. A reporter described how billionaire venture capitalist, Peter Hoffer's private plane crashed landed into the Pacific off the coast of California.

Hoffer and five of the six other people on board escaped with no injuries. A twenty-eight-year-old woman was the only casualty, a search was launched but her body was never found. An image of Abby briefly flashed on the screen.

My phone rang all night, many sobbing over the loss of Abby. I faked an air of sorrow. My memory then went to the encounter with the stranger in the bar. I had passed it off as only an illusion, a vision concocted by a man who couldn't hold his liquor. Had it really happened?

It was three AM before I finally got to bed. I reached to turn off the light on the nightstand. I saw a card resting on the polished wood, the card with only three words. A red check mark had been added.

Chapter 13: At the Symphony
Written by Mela Saylor

Concert Hall
Symphony Orchestra
2017

Miranda and Astrid had tickets to hear the symphony Saturday night, but now Astrid wouldn't go. She insisted on staying home to keep an eye on 'Buzz', the timefly she found Thursday night.

"Take Rowena with you, she'd enjoy that," Astrid insisted. And now it was Miranda and Rowena who sat in the concert hall listening to the orchestra warming up before their performance.

This was a special occasion as the symphony, along with a special guest conductor, was playing a never before heard concertina from a now-deceased, but just discovered Norwegian Composer. The hall was rapidly filling to capacity and by the time the orchestra finished warming up, there was a palpable silent air of expectation that fell over the audience.

The lights darkened as the conductor walked on stage to a thunderous and lengthy applause. He bowed then turned to the orchestra and raised his baton.

Music flowed seamlessly without effort and filled the hall with the magical sounds, mesmerizing everyone. Throughout the first half of the performance, Miranda noticed that Rowena kept glancing at her program, squinting in the semi darkness. She nudged her and whispered.

"What's wrong?"

"Nothing, I'm just trying to figure out who the composer is. I've never heard anything like this before."

"Edvard Grieg, a Norwegian composer – this particular piece is being played for the first time tonight." Miranda noticed they were starting to get dirty looks from the people around them that were annoyed with their talking. She suspected Rowena had never been there before because she was busy looking at everything around them except the orchestra. It was a beautiful place, Miranda had to concede.

It wasn't until after the intermission that the trouble began. When the lights darkened again and the music started swelling, Miranda caught a whiff of what she would later call a cross between lightening and silk. She turned to Rowena to mention it and found her looking up at the ceiling. On the ceiling of the concert hall was a congregation of a few hundred lightening bugs crawling around, lighting up sporadically.

"Look – what a pretty display, Miranda." This sight seemed to be more interesting to Rowena than the music, Miranda noticed. Then she looked at them again. The lights on these insects were not the typical warm yellow lights that were found on lightening bugs. The lights on the insects over their heads were larger and a cold silver-violet light. Their shape was different, too.

"Oh no…", Miranda whispered. She looked around her. Very few people noticed these so far – but these insects seemed to be swarming the ceiling and their numbers growing while the orchestra played on, oblivious to it all.

Halfway through the third movement, an insect made its way to the conductor and flew to perch on the end of the conductor's baton. The conductor, momentarily startled, stopped for a moment in surprise. And the orchestra stopped playing. The audience took note and sat up to see what was going on. The orchestra began again with the conductor. Then the fly moved forward on his baton. The conductor ignored it until it crawled up to his hand. In his attempt to get rid of the fly, the conductor moved his baton with vigor. The orchestra played more forcefully. Some in the audience closer to the stage covered their ears. Then the fly screeched at the conductor and flew off his baton only to come back and fly around his head. The conductor jumped back a foot in surprise, but quickly recovered his composure and continued. The next time the fly landed on his baton and emitted a piercing shriek. The conductor started falling, and his flailing arms attempted to right himself. His mouth opened and closed in surprise, as he teetered on the precipice of the platform. It all happened so slowly it was like watching a movie in slow-motion. Someone in the audience cracked their chewing gum and a cell phone went off somewhere. A small flash of light reverberated from around the conductor and suddenly he was back on the podium conducting the orchestra not missing a beat as if nothing had happened.

"Did you just see that?" Miranda whispered to a bug-eyed Rowena.

"I – I think so. But I don't understand what just happened. What happened, dear? And I don't think anyone in the audience noticed it. It was pretty obvious that something bizarre just happened, don't you think? Please tell me what happened."

"You're right... "

And a very surprised conductor jumped back a foot once again. He started falling, this time his flailing arms vigorously flapping by his side still clutching the baton. His mouth opened and closed in surprise as he teetered in the precipice of falling onto his backside. Someone in the audience cracked their gum and a cell phone went off somewhere.

"Wait for it again. . ." Miranda put her hand on Rowena's arm, looking around. "Watch what that timefly does." There it was again – that light that reverberated from around the conductor.

"Ok … I saw that .. but what is it?"

"I believe that was a time ripple – sort of like a hiccup in time. Time is trying to right itself somewhere. Someone, somewhere, at some point in time right now, is trying to make things right – and I have a strong hunch it has to do with that little bugger Astrid is sitting with. I think she's attached to our little Buzz. You know she named that thing, don't you?"

"But why are we the only ones who can see this happening?" Rowena asked, looking around.

"Because we are children of the Borealis, we are gifted with the ability to be more attuned to nature and all its vibrations. We see into the beyond.

And for the third and final time, the conductor started falling. This time he was successful and finally met the floor with a resounding crash. There was a tremendous burst of energy that flashed from around him in an arc and then all the timeflies took off. They left the building within minutes. In all the hullabaloo, no one noticed their departure, as they were instantly called home to a world they never knew.

Chapter 14: The Fly in The Ointment
Written by Eleni Byrnes

Local County Hospital
1950s

"Now tell me, how do you feel--what are your real feelings? Hm...and why do you think you feel this way about that?"

Ah, here I was, once again, at one of the dreaded "sessions", where some annoying man asks condescendingly pointless questions in his bored voice. His eyes stared ominously at me from behind horn-rimmed, thick lensed glasses that were always sliding down his nose on a pasty face. He blinked several times uncontrollably. The "Doctor" was a follower of the Freudian approach and was always asking inappropriately outrageous questions of a highly personal nature.

In vain I once again attempted to make myself comfortable, as I reclined on the derelict piece of furniture that passed as a sofa. It was upholstered in some drab scratchy industrial type of material which was stained and had lumpy stuffing that had a faint musty smell. Inwardly cringing, I wondered just as I had during every session, the number of people who must have lain upon it and to what degree they practiced their hygiene. To make matters even worse, on humid days, it stank. As soon as every session was over I begged the nurse for permission to take a shower.

I could see no benefit of participating in these loathsome psycho-babble sessions and could not wait until the mandatory hour was over. The whole time I gave answers, he sweated profusely, to the point of grabbing a handkerchief from his coat pocket and mopping his face. He always remained seated, dwarfed behind an elaborate wooden desk, his pen scratching out on paper, making notes of everything I said. And I could feel my stomach lurch and my pulse raise in horror, as I wondered

What in heaven's name, what sort of atrocities could he be writing? Also on the desk were a typewriter, notebooks, and a brass bell on its surface, which he would officiously ring at the beginning and end of each session. Naturally, I found him quite repellent and intimidating and could only manage to meekly nod, give a shake of the head, or utter a monosyllable in an attempt to answer, as he pretended to be encouraging and supportive by displaying a grey-toothed smile.

Always I would be caught off guard by the fireplace wall of the office on which hung a watercolor seascape under glass, and upon the mantle lay a large piece of driftwood. The part of me that had been struggling to resurface, would suddenly sink. I could feel myself becoming smaller and retreating back into that same dark, safe place, upon seeing that damned driftwood and seascape mocking me. Bringing back every emotion to be relived of the last time I saw my former love. We had been collecting odd shells and pieces of driftwood on the beach. How he loved to talk and dream of a future together while never acting on any of it, he was good at spinning dreams and castles in the sky. Obviously, my heart was to be neither respected, nor spared from the idiosyncrasies of his grand self-delusions, and finally having enough of unkept promises, I had decided to end the relationship abruptly. Quite naturally in the process of dealing with such grief, I had lost a good twenty or so pounds. My once lustrous long brown hair hung lankly down my back, but slowly I had begun the process of reclaiming some vestige of my former self. This time it was just too much to bear, I could not help myself, spying the brass bell on that man's desk, I snatched it up, hurled it at the painting. Glass shattered, and time seemed to stand still as the shards momentarily froze, sparkling like diamonds in mid-air, before falling in sharp pieces to the floor. Momentarily the man was shaken and taken aback in shock, then he took a deep breath. At that precise moment, an unusual fly that I had observed buzzing about appeared. For some reason it seemed to be in the habit of following me down the halls, and sometimes it accompanied me to these ridiculous sessions, often it liked pacing across the glass over the watercolor painting. Perhaps it considered itself an art critic and liked ocean scenes. Who knows?

Now in his office, this fly who I had come to consider as some type of ally, landed directly on his nose, and I laughed aloud at the sight of his eyes crossing as they focused on the insect offender, as he sputtered in outrage that it had dared to alight on the tip of his greasy nose. I knew the punishment that would surely come next, but it was worth it and extremely amusing to see him thrown off kilter and show any sort of emotion for just once. I found myself snickering at the ridiculousness of it all: where I was--the man--his voice-- his office and that fly perched on his nose was just the icing on the cake!

This fly who had been happily buzzing it's way throughout the institution for about a week or so now, had done what I had for so long dreamed to do: knock Dr. Friedrich Von Schmidt off the pedestal he kept himself on.

"Dammit, Confound It, Blast It All!" The Dr was a secret germaphobe and had an especially severe phobia about flies. He grabbed his handkerchief to rub the spot where the fly had been. It may have been my imagination, but while it had been on his nose, it actually turned around and looked right at me. It rubbed its front legs together in the manner of a villain

117

who rubs his hands together whilst uttering "mwuahaha" as it winked one of its silvery gear-like eyes at me. There was a high-pitched keening noise as its iridescent wings vibrated before it took itself off to flight.

Naturally by this time, it was about all I could do not to fall off my chair and mirthfully roll on the floor, so I held my sides as I found myself gripped by an uncontrollable laughter .

"Hahaha! Oh, this has to be one of the most hilarious things I have ever seen." I just could not stop laughing and if you had ever met the man you would also have had the same reaction.

"Miss Salazar, please contain yourself, now calm down.. tsk."

The result of which, had the opposite effect, and only caused me to break into even more fits of hysterical laughter by that time. Shaking his head in disapproval, this annoying man with the bored voice rang for the nurse.

"Miss Salazar's medication treatment plan does not appear to be working, the twice daily Valium dosage of 5 milligrams must be upped to three times a day at 7.5 milligrams, but we will keep the Lithium dosage the same, a re-evaluation may be necessary, enter this into the patient's chart. For now, I prescribe and recommend a Chlorpromazine injection be given after she has been escorted to her room."

The nurse busily took notes and afterwards returned to her station. Finally I had had enough. Something rose up within me and my eyes narrowed in anger at how casually he displayed such arrogant pomposity in his treatment of me as a patient. What utter unmitigated gall!

"I am not having an episode, you cannot keep me drugged up over having a sense of humor, doctor. And I defy you to even try it, you loathsome, vile little man." I was surprised to find my voice rising in anger as I suddenly rose up from the sofa with eyes narrowed. The walls I had been hiding behind had fallen, and the spark that had remained waiting deep within me had begun to blaze.

Suddenly my ally had come back and decided to dive-bomb the good doctor. Indeed I had become quite weary of his probing into my innermost psyche and derived a sadistic pleasure at seeing him discombobulated to such a degree. In reaction there was a great deal of dramatic flailing about, and after a few moments of this, his hand contacted the fly and smacked it so hard it landed in his glass. The poor thing struggled to keep afloat, finally finding a secure footing on top of an ice cube.

After an intermittent time, it crawled up to the edge of the glass, and I could swear that I heard a tiny hiccup as it unsteadily crawled along the rim. It shook itself like a dog, and with its little legs carefully groomed its eyes before taking off. A high-pitched keening noise emanated as it flew, escalating until my head throbbed, as it flew in a staggered pattern until it ran right into the surface of the painting with a "ping". During the span of a few seconds, the fly and painting had simultaneously illuminated, colors swirling then parted to reveal a long tentacle sinuously arising up from the watery depths that churned wildly, as clouds scuttled across an ever-darkening sky.

Lightning flashed across the sky in the painting, "D-di-did you see that? Something is moving - there in the painting, and the sky, I could swear I saw lightning," stuttered the doctor.

"Why no, I see nothing, merely the painting itself, and have no idea what you are talking about doctor". Ah, how remarkable, he finally he shows a bit of emotion in his voice. I had indeed seen and had absolutely no intention of letting on that I had. It would be satisfying to see him on the other end of the power and control spectrum and be the one questioning his own sanity.

The suckers of a dark tentacle were visible as it snaked its way from out of the borders of the painting, lightning flashed again highlighting its skin. The beginning of a blood curdling scream was
 cut off as it wrapped around the doctor's body, and completely covered his mouth. All that could be seen of his face were eyes that bulged out in horror. And just as quickly as it had snaked out of the painting, the tentacle withdrew, hauling Dr Von Schmidt out of his chair, and down into the depths of the churning waters which suddenly stilled, leaving no trace of what had just happened. The painting was as before, a seascape watercolor under glass. I remained frozen in place seated, such was my surprise at what had just happened. My tormentor was now gone.

Again, I heard an intense high-pitched keening that caused my skull to vibrate and ache when the fly grazed my ear upon passing. I raised my hands to my ears and closed my eyes, when I opened them, I was back on the beach with my fiancé at the exact moment when I had broken the engagement. Such was my disbelief that I had thought it to be some hallucination, due to the inexplicable events that had taken place earlier in the doctor's office. I sniffed the air and felt the sand under my bare feet, wriggled my toes in it and knew it was real. Looking at my now ex-fiancé, and how the shock registered on his face at having our engagement called off, I felt a new sensation - Freedom.

I gathered my bag up, turned my back on him and walked away. The fly, my ally, had given me a second chance that must not be wasted.

One of the first things I did was have a jeweler melt down the engagement ring and make a brooch in the shape of a fly, with a diamond body and emerald eyes.

Background for chapter 15:

The four of them materialize together June 15ᵗʰ, 2017, and not sure how long they will be in this time period, they agree they should take separate accommodations so not to arouse any undue concerns in their communities about four strangers suddenly appearing out of nowhere. Edward rents a room in a B&B in Navarre as a retired history professor and starts up the "club" so everyone can meet there. Reggie rents a room in downtown Canton, and Dorothy and Elizabeth get a room together in North Canton.

Chapter 15: BUGGERS
(Sequel to Applejack)

Written by Edward Klink

Fort Laurens, Bolivar, Ohio
Saturday, June 24, 2017

It's Saturday, June 24, 2017, and a little over four months since the Applejack incident. Our four amateur historians are in a car heading for Fort Laurens in Bolivar to try to discern the name of an unknown soldier from the Revolutionary War by finding the names of soldiers in his company. They could then investigate these names and hometowns to see if there is a pattern of families and use this information to close in on the identity of the unknown.

Dorothy begins to speak as their car turns west on Route #212 off Interstate #77, "I am still amazed that no one has believed us about what happened in Navarre, over four months ago now. I almost don't believe myself, except that yesterday while I was at the library doing research on Fort Laurens, I noticed a picture of the guy who killed McKinley and it was the same person we saw in front of the De Fine Building. I don't forget faces and it proves to me that we weren't dreaming."

"How is it that no matter what we're doing, we always end up back on this timefly subject?" Reggie looked out the window at the passing landscape. "But you know that's all I think about too, and I had myself convinced that we somehow all dreamed the same dream because we were all at the same table and had eaten lunch at that roast beef place on south Cleveland Avenue, before we went to Navarre. Maybe we had food poisoning, but we weren't sick when we got there, and there was something in that jar."

"I haven't been able to believe it myself and am going to look at that picture on my new I-Phone," Elizabeth tuned on her I-Phone, touches Safari and types in 'Leon Czolgosc.' Up pops the same face she saw in Navarre. Her eyes widen and tears form as her unprovable truth becomes provable to her. "Look," she says and holds her phone up for all to see.

Reggie pulls into the Marathon gas station and parks.

Edward looks and says, "That's proof for me."

They all just look at each other and say in unison, "Those little BUGGERS are real."

Reggie speaks up, "All this time I've been trying to disprove this to myself and you guys just proved it to be true. We were all there and we did see Leon and we almost saved McKinley."

"No," says Edward, "That would be a Paradox. You can't go back in Time and change anything."

"You can't go back in Time," says Reggie, "but we did, so how can you say, we can't change anything?"

"You're right," says Dorothy, "we already did one impossible thing, why not two?"

"Those "timeflies" must be real," says Reggie, "and I would bet that their genus is "Drosophila Melangaster, or vinegar flies."

"Wow," says Elizabeth, "how do you know all of that?"

"What?" asked Reggie.

"That big name," says Elizabeth.

"It's just a description of the bug," says Reggie.

"Well, what does it look like?" says Elizabeth.

"Their bodies are small," says Reggie, "and they have red eyes, but I'm describing a fruit fly because of what we know already. They like fermented apple juice and I think that our 'Time Flies' must be a subspecies of that."

"Fort Laurens is just around the corner," says Edward, "let's go."

Reggie pulls back onto #212 and stops at the light with his left turn signal on. The light changes and they turn left. There are only ten or twelve homes on the left before they reach Fort Lauren. They all stare at the entrance and try to imagine the winter of January, 1779, and Simon Girty, the British agent and his small group of Seneca-Cayuga Indians reconnoitering the defenses of the fort and noticing the deplorable conditions and ambushing sixteen militiamen just south of where their car is and mutilating two of them in full sight of the Fort.

"Those militiamen must have been brave and patriotic," thought Elizabeth.

I'm glad those timeflies didn't bring us here, thought Reggie.

Edward and Dorothy just closed their eyes and imagined the coldness and the hunger those men must have felt.

Reggie pulls into the parking lot and parks with each of them immersed in their thoughts of what happened here two hundred thirty-eight years ago.

"What if we could control those flies?" Reggie wondered aloud, staring into space.

"What flies?" asks Elizabeth.

"Those "timeflies," says Reggie.

"Why?" asks Dorothy.

Reggie thinks to himself; *I can almost hear all of our thoughts as we observe this place and know the tragedy that happened here.*

"What if we could help?" Reggie mused, giving voice to the possibility of a divine intervention. "What if we could warn those sixteen people about Simon Girty? What if we could get those flies to get us back to January 1779 while we were standing in the middle of Fort Laurens and we each had a picnic basket full of food and maybe a blanket or two under our arms?"

"Great thoughts," says Edward, "but how do we do that? Are we just going to go out and catch some timeflies and dart in and out of every tragedy in history?"

"I did some research on Google and in the library," says Elizabeth, "and can find no reference to time travel except maybe in some early petroglyphs by American Indians in northern Arizona. I was just learning to read petroglyphs and figured they must be high on Locoweed. I noticed little figures by their fire and fruit drawings and got a magnifying glass to look closer at the photographs and noticed what I thought were smudges but could see winged little creatures with lines in the stone emanating from a center like a hot coal or light, but those lines could indicate sound."

"You never told us this before," says Dorothy. "But don't you remember hearing the music they make each time we disappear in and out of time?"

"It hasn't been important until now," says Elizabeth, "What if we can learn to control them?"

"We have to catch some before we can control them," says Reggie. "That sound that they make must amplify like radiation which makes every piece of flesh nearby vibrate, making the living flesh not able to see the real fly."

"We could ask Jack," says Dorothy, "if he has any more Applejack?"

"Jack said that that was the only jar," says Reggie. "I wonder if he still has that opened jar we had? It might give us a clue."

"I have it," says Edward.

"What?" asks Reggie.

"That night that Navarre happened to us, Jack was very impressed with your talk, and gave the rest of the Applejack to me. I was saving it for us to party some evening."

"Where is it?" asks Reggie.

"At home," Edward grins.

"There could be some juvenile pupae in that jar," says Reggie.

They all look at each other and say at the same time, "Let's go get it."

Half an hour later they were in Edward's apartment. Reggie parks, and they follow Edward into his kitchen. Opening the cupboard door under the sink, Edward retrieves the jar and hands it to Reggie. It's still half full and the metal lid is screwed on tight. Reggie holds it up to the light and peers into the darkness of the liquid inside the jar.

"There are some specks in there," says Reggie and takes it over to the kitchen table which is flooded with sunlight. They sit at the table and watch as Reggie holds it up to the brightest patch of sunlight.

"There's definitely something in there," Reggie observed as he shook the jar and held it to his ear. "There's a slight sound. Can you hear it?"

"How will we know if it's the timeflies?" asks Edward, peering into the seemingly empty jar.

"I remember what happened when I first opened that jar," says Reggie, "but more than that, I remember looking into the sides of that jar before I opened it and saw the same things that I see now, but now there are a lot more of them. I think, what we have here is a super incubator and this Applejack must be the perfect environment. Everything I know about this rare breed of fly tells me that we have a jar full of time travel."

"I think that each time we open this lid," says Reggie excitedly, thumping the lid with his index finger, "a new generation exits, and a single pair of this type of fly is capable of producing thousands of generations and will as long as this Applejack lasts."

"We're history nuts, right?" asked Elizabeth, "I say we have fun and go fix something! So what's our first mission?"

"We can't have any mission until we understand how this power works," says Reggie. "It appears natural, so there must be a logical explanation. How close we must be to intercept these sound waves with the vibration of our bodies, and how did those flies know to take us back 238 years, and not 237 or 239 or just a day or just one second?"

"We must be a part of that equation," says Edward.

"I think so too," says Elizabeth, "I've often thought that our mind produces waves when we think and that these time flies must have antenna to understand these waves, at least where time and history intersect."

"You might be on to something, Elizabeth," says Reggie, "because quantum mechanics has proven that space and time are the same thing, and that matter can be in two places at the same time. I don't think that it was accidental that, when we arrived at the DeFine Building in Navarre, we were all thinking about McKinley and my talk was about Leon Czolgosc. Right before our travel back in time, I was wondering about Leon and if he ever visited that place."

"That must have been it," says Edward, "those little 'BUGGERS' were tuned in to us and that might have been the only time in 'Space Time' that Czolgosc ever visited that place and those bugs connected our thoughts to coincide with 'Space Time'.

"But how did the timeflies know to bring us back to 2017?" asks Reggie.

"When the event was over, after we chased Czolgosc back to the train tracks, the coincidence in time was over." "The "timeflies" stopped being the catalyst and time returned to normal," says Edward.

"That sounds logical," says Dorothy, "but none of this is provable as a scientific fact."

"You're right," says Reggie.

"And since this is just a theorem," says Edward, "and we've figured how it happened, all we have to do is follow the process we were a part of in Navarre and see if we get the same results. If we do, Theorem becomes fact."

"Sounds scary to me," says Elizabeth.

"Me too," says Dorothy.

"You mean, we would have to go to the J. D. DeFine Building, and try to think the same thoughts we thought then," says Elizabeth, "and open that bottle of Applejack?"

"Yeah," says Edward, "same input, same outcome, we hope. It's the only way to prove that the past still exists."

"Too deep for me," says Dorothy.

"I think I have a better idea," says Reggie, "Fort Laurens and those sixteen militiamen that got ambushed by Simon Girty and his Indian buddies."

"What do you mean?", says Edward.

"They know the location of the ambush, and have erected a marker at that spot," says Reggie, "just south of the fort. I'll take the jar of Applejack and timeflies to that memorial and think about the two militiamen that got killed and open the jar. You guys stand back and watch, and if I go back in time to 1779, warn them and return to 2017. I should only disappear for a short time, because Mr. Evans said that we never moved when he returned with the glasses for drinking the Applejack.

We were the only ones who knew that anything had happened, so I'll signal you when it's over and you can come to me."

"Sounds too dangerous to me," says Edward.

"I think we should all go, or no one goes," says Dorothy.

"Me too," says Elizabeth.

"What do you think, Reggie?" asks Edward.

"We were all there the first time," says Reggie, "and I'm glad you all were there, because otherwise I would have believed that I was mentally ill."

"We all felt that way," says Dorothy, "until today."

"I think Fort Laurens would be a good test," says Elizabeth.

"You've got to remember," says Edward, "that the Revolutionary War was a full fight, and no war is chivalrous. Simon Girty was a savage man and the Indians with him were as savage as him. They scalped those militiamen and hacked them to pieces in front of those soldiers at the fort and dared them to come out and rescue them."

"I think it's worth a try," says Reggie, as empathy invades his mind.

"All lives are worth saving," says Edward.

"When do we leave?" asks Elizabeth.

"When is our paper due on the identity of that unknown soldier?" asks Dorothy.

"Next Friday," answers Elizabeth.

"Then let's do it tomorrow," says Dorothy.

"I know it's the month of June," says Reggie, "and warm but we better wear some warm clothes because remember, we're headed for February 1779 and it was brutally cold."

They're excited as they approve the plan, which is that Reggie will pick them up tomorrow at 11:00 A M at the Stark County Library on Market North in Canton. Each is to be dressed for cold weather.

Reggie arrives and they leave for Fort Laurens.

128

"Earmuffs in June?" chuckles Edward to Dorothy as they smile at the way each other is dressed, with insulated underwear, heavy coats, and scarves.

"That winter hat makes your nose red," says Dorothy.

"That's just my excitement for today," says Edward, "to see if the timeflies will really do what we want them to."

"I'm not going to tell you guys," says Reggie, "what to think when we open that Applejack, until right before, so that we won't think any extraneous thoughts, and get the correct 'Time Space Past' to warn those people."

Reggie turned on the air conditioner to keep them cool until they got to Fort Laurens. Their eyes were bright as they engaged in small talk keeping their minds off the realization that they were pioneers of 'Inner Space Time Travel'.

Reggie turned west on Route #212, from Interstate #77 to the dead end and turned south. Fort Laurens is only a quarter mile away and in less than a minute they turn into the entrance. This is Sunday and they are the only ones there. Reggie parked the car and points to the Granite Monument, supposed to be the location of the massacre. They get out and follow Reggie, with Edward carrying the timeflies in the Applejack jar. They stand next to the monument as close as they can get. Edward places the jar on the rock in the center and they gather around. It's a hot day in June and they are sweating in winter clothes as Reggie explains the plight of those soldiers that are right there 237 years and 6 months in the past.

"They're cold and hungry and have just come outside the main southern gate of the fort to gather firewood. They can't even take their Muskets because they are low on powder and ammunition. They don't know that outside these fort walls, there is terror on every side, and are miserable from hunger and cold weather."

The monument is smaller than the table at the J. D. DeFine Building and they are outside instead of inside when comparing today, to the beginning of their first Time Journey in Navarre. Reggie is at the far end of the stone and looks everybody in the eye and asked them.

"What are you thinking?"

They respond together, "The cold, the hunger, the sixteen soldiers."

Reggie listens and is satisfied as he lifts the Applejack jar, thinking, *I'll bet Simon Girty won't like this*, as he unscrews the metal lid on the jar. The sharp bouquet of apples rise first in the heat off the monument followed by a very high-pitched buzzing sound which make their senses react to the vibration. They remembered this sensation from before.

"It's working." Dorothy squinted her eyes and saw Reggie disintegrating.

The heat turns to bitter cold as the four of them reintegrate standing, facing each other. The rock monument is gone, and they are standing at the bottom of a small hill next to a frozen creek in the middle of a forest. The trees are huge.

They are in the middle of a hardwood forest, oaks, hickory, and maple. Then they hear screaming and shouting permeate the crisp coldness and winds.

They look toward the sound and see a group of shabbily dressed men with only sticks in their hands and blankets over their shoulders, trying to defend themselves against one very big white man and eight ferocious looking Indians, each wielding a knife and tomahawk.

The battle is all one sided until the attackers see the four strangers appear out of nowhere, behind the militiamen they are attacking. The Indians stop immediately in fear, knowing that something miraculous just happened and Simon Girty wonders to himself how these reinforcements arrived so quickly. The Indians are frightened, and Simon Girty is intensely angry as he refocuses his attack on the newcomers. With tomahawk raised in his right hand, knife in his left hand,

and guttural growls escaping his throat, he rushes the front man of this new group, Reggie.

"Run toward the fort," yells Reggie, as he picks up a tree limb to protect himself from this onrushing bull of a man.

They run, because Reggie told them to, but then as one, they pick up a tree limb and rush back toward the attacker to help Reggie.

Simon's tomahawk is descending for a murderous blow to Reggie's head, with Reggie trying to parry the blow with his tree limb. A loud high-pitched buzzing sound vibrates through the forest and the reinforcements disintegrate before the astonished eyes of Simon Girty. Simon's tomahawk cuts deeply into the tree limb where just a second ago, an enemy's head with glaring eyes was opposing him. This is the trusted British agent, sent to reconnoiter this fort for an attack by the British to destroy this American dream of independence. Simon is bewildered because he doesn't believe in ghosts and thinks to himself, *These Americans must have a new secret weapon, and I don't know how to fight it.* The Indians run over to him and with hand signs and the language of the Seneca and Cayuga tell him that the Great Spirit had intervened and saved this fort. Two soldiers are slaughtered and thirteen of the militiamen make it back to the fort. One is still alive from the battle and kept prisoner by Simon to be interrogated about this new secret weapon of moving troops invisibly.

~

A young girl on a bicycle, and a chipmunk on the monument, are watching a strange sight of four reintegrating people appearing around this granite monument with a jar of amber liquid and metal lid laying on the stone. Reggie regained his senses first and replaced the lid on the jar. The young girl on the bicycle thinks that her eyes just played a trick on her and the chipmunk runs away, happy that these people didn't get the acorns, in his cheek pouches, saved from last fall. Sunshine and warmth envelope these four shivering beings as all senses return.

"Are we all O K?" asks Reggie.

"Are you O K?" asks Edward. "That guy was trying to cut your head off."

"The timeflies made him miss," says Reggie, "and the rest of you look fine, maybe a little frost bitten."

"We didn't save those guys," says Elizabeth.

"We failed," says Dorothy.

"I don't think so," says Reggie. "Didn't you guys notice that Simon and those Indians were a superior force and knocking those militiamen down with every parry? The four in front were the offense and the back five were doing the scalping and savagery. If we hadn't shown up, I think all of them would have been killed."

"You mean, we might have saved those thirteen?" asks Elizabeth.

"That's exactly what I mean," says Reggie, "and the way you guys came back to help me completely stopped their offense and gained appreciation for the American defensive fighting spirit."

"I have proof that we saved them," says Reggie.

"What proof?" asks Elizabeth.

"Look at your history books," says Reggie, "they all say that only two died but we all saw that they all would have died, except for our appearance."

"Shouldn't one of us write a journal of what happened today?" asks Edward.

"That would be a good idea," says Elizabeth.

"Someone already has," says Reggie.

"Who?" asked Elizabeth.

"He's one of those 'timefly' writers by the name of Ed Klink.

"Let's get back to Canton," Edward says, "we still have a paper to research and write on that unknown soldier."

"That was still scary," says Dorothy, as they head back for the parking lot.

Chapter 16: Back at the Clock Shop
Written by Mela Saylor

Lake Cable, Ohio
Saturday, August 10th, 2020

This is getting old, Dottie thought as she materialized once more. She stood and looked around to get her bearings. She couldn't afford to run into Vincent again. The thought of him made her break into a cold sweat. She scolded herself – *think of Reginald.*

This time Dottie was on the edge of a golf course. She heard some peculiar sounds and found herself at the side of a busy road. Cars and other motorized vehicles whizzed by at speeds she never thought they could go! Horns blared as she neared the road and she jumped back to safety beside the trees. *Is this what that other road I saw in 2027 was for? Heavens – there's a lot of people here!* She eyed the five lanes of traffic and wondered how she was going to cross it. After a while, the traffic thinned out and she was able to run across holding her skirt up in front of her with two hands. She was positive Thomas was somewhere in that large complex of buildings over there. She looked around and found most of them were closed up for the night. She started to leave in a panic but saw 8:20 Clock Shop painted on a column on the side of the building, with an arrow to a small door in the side. She looked in the door window at an empty poorly lit hallway and opened the door. She tiptoed down and found another door with light streaming out. The place was locked. Then she saw some movement inside. She pounded on the door.

"Let me in, Thomas!" He didn't hear her? She pounded some more. "Thomas!"

"I'm coming! I'm coming – and I've got a gun!" Thomas threatened the would-be intruder by waving a gun in the air as he peaked through the window and squinted, his eyes widening when he recognized her. He hurriedly opened the door and Dottie rushed in, hugging him desperately.

"I'm so glad to see you, Thomas! How have you been?"

"Dang tired of waiting for you to show up, you little twit! All I have to say is that it's about time." He deadbolted the door behind her to turn and slowly walk, with a distinct limp in his gait, to the back of the shop. As Dottie followed him, she noticed how frail he was and that he now used a cane.

"It sure is about time," Dottie smiled wryly. For the first time in what seemed an eternity, she was able to relax and take a deep breath. Dottie sat down amidst the silent shop. "Do you have anything to drink around here?" She was parched and her ears were ringing.

Thomas reached under his desk pulling out a bottle of whisky and poured each of them a glass. She raised her eyebrows and glass in a silent toast.

"Not exactly what I was going for, but it'll do. When did you take up drinking?"

Thomas raised his stone-grey eyebrows and winked. "Probably the second week I was put here -so it's been a while."

"Oh wow – hey kitty." An orange tabby slinked into the room and circled Thomas's legs, glancing at Dottie curiously.

"You're not taking the cat – she's mine now," Thomas gruffly stated.

"This isn't Cora, is it?" Dottie's eye widened in amazement. "But it's not possible. Cats don't live that long!" Dottie started calculating the years. "If she was just a year old

135

in 1921 and it's now 2020 – that would make this cat one hundred years old! How weird is that?" Thomas was shuffling toward a back corner when he heard that last comment from Dottie. He stopped and turned around, looking at her in amazement. He waved his finger in the air.

"I'm tied to this shop, time has stopped, you are time-traveling and doing god only knows what – and you call an old cat weird? Sheesh."

Thomas turned and slowly made his way to a side desk in his shop, moving it around, he opened a secret compartment. Laying there was the Internal Vibration Frequency Meter he had made.

"How does it work?"

"This," he said, "is it. All that needs to be done is blow in this and all the flies will come back."

"All of them?"

"Every single one. You'll have to get out of the way and let them in. It could take a while since those damned things are everywhere." He leaned in and whispered to her.

"Personally, I think they've already screwed up history, so to speak. But we'll probably never know, will we?" He took it out of her hand. "Remember where I'm putting it – can you do that?"

"But I have just one question." Dottie asked, remembering there were several holes in it. "Which one of those –"

Then she felt her feet tingling again. Before she could open her mouth and finish her question, she disappeared.

Chapter 17: The Mission
Written by Ron Luikart

Fort Bragg, Tennessee
2012/1862

Sergeant Mike Holt knelt in the open door of an old C-47 waiting for the green light to blink on. When it did, he and his squad of fifteen men would jump from the plane like they had done many times before. The only things keeping that from happening was a red light and the fact that they were still ten minutes from the drop zone. The view from Holt's position never ceased to amaze him. He had been in the Army for twenty-five years and a paratrooper most of that time, and still the minutes before a jump were always the best time for him. It was peaceful as he surveyed the scene. The sky was starting to brighten as the sun inched into the eastern sky. The landscape below started to show details and take on a patchwork quilt look, and white clouds drifted by. They had left Fort Bragg to take part in maneuvers in Tennessee. Pretty simple mission. Drop in, simulate blowing up a bridge, get picked up, and return to Bragg in time to throw down some beers at the NCO club. He was looking forward to NCO club. Before he let the barracks for the mission, he had double checked his calendar. April 7, 2012. His retirement date was in two days. This jump was to be his last jump, just for old time sakes.

A red, blinking light brought Holt back into the plane.

"Stand and face the door!" he shouted above the engine and wind noise.

Fifteen soldiers with bulky chutes and equipment struggled to stand and face him.

The light turned to a blinking green.

"Hook up and check equipment!"

Static lines clicked into place on the steel cable that ran fore and aft along the ceiling of the plane. Each trooper checked their gear and the equipment of the man in front of him. When they were finished, they all looked at Holt to indicate that they were ready.

The light stopped blinking and became a steady green.

The gear for the mission was the first to go. Holt pushed the skid out the door and leaned out to watch it fall. Fifty feet below the plane, the static line jerked taut and pulled the chutes from their packs. The gear swung gently underneath the chutes and descended toward the ground.

Holt faced his men.

"Go!" he commanded.

Each man waddled to the door and jumped into the morning air. Corporal Dan Wilson was the last man in line, and Holt slapped him on the back as he went by.

"See ya' downstairs!"

Wilson gave him a thumbs up as he went through the door. Out of habit, Holt looked back into the plane, just to double check. It was empty, except for him and the pilots, so he faced the door and jumped.

The quietness and the feeling of being suspended for the next several seconds were what he really enjoyed about being a paratrooper. It was like being in a dream that he wanted to go on forever. But, right on schedule his chute exploded from its pack and cracked open above him. He swung like a pendulum until he gained control of his body's oscillation and settled into his decent. He looked down and saw that the gear had landed, and he could still see the white canopies of the men who had gone before. Routine. That's what he liked.

He did notice, however, that the cloud cover had changed. They were thicker and much closer together than when they had jumped. He had been trained to avoid clouds because of the dangers of collisions and vertigo, but he had ignored the warnings and had found going through clouds quite exhilarating. Several hundred feet below, he saw Wilson trying to maneuver around a cloud that was coming in from his right. He didn't make and disappeared into its thickness.

"What the hell!" Holt shouted and followed Wilson.

The coolness of clouds had always refreshed him, but this one was different. He felt the cold as soon as his feet and legs penetrated it. It was numbing and it soon enveloped him. Then he heard the sound of insects. *"This high up? That's weird," He thought.* There was a ringing in his ears and then the strong stench of mildew began to suffocate him. He became dizzy, and then he vomited.

Earth smells battled with the pungent mildew and the sour smell of vomit. Finally, the smell of grass and leaves won, and Holt became aware that he was lying face down on the ground. Warm sun beat on his back. A far-off voice called his name. He rolled over and the bright sun knifed into his eyes and his head began to pound. A form stood over him and blocked the sun. He blinked hard several times and finally the form became Wilson.

"You O.K., Sarge?"

"What happened?"

"Dunno, Sarge. You O.K.?"

"Just give me minute," Holt replied, as he sat up and looked around.

They had landed in a wooded area. All was quiet. No birds. No breeze. Nothing.

"Where's the gear and the rest of the guys?" Holt asked.

"Couldn't find 'em."

"Let's spread out and look for them," Holt said, as he stood on wobbly legs. "They have to be around here somewhere."

Wilson went off in one direction as Holt took a drink from his canteen. He glanced at his watch and saw that it said 6:30. "Strange," he thought, "that it would be 6:30 with the sun directly overhead." He checked the watch to see if it were still running, and it was.

"Sarge! Sarge! Over here!"

Holt jogged in the direction of Wilson's voice and found him standing at the bottom of a gully next to a dead horse.

"Look at this, Sarge. It has a broken leg, and somebody shot it. I found this too," Wilson said, as he held up a spent cartridge. "What do ya' make of it?"

"Doesn't look like any cartridge that I've ever seen," Holt replied.

From the distance they heard a low rumble.

"Sound like thunder," Wilson said.

"Can't be. There's not a cloud in the sky."

Holt took a map from his case and spread it on the ground. According to the map, they should have been in a meadow. They weren't. The map showed the terrain to be level with no hill for ten miles or so, but this ground was hilly.

"Son of a bitch, we got dropped in the wrong place," Wilson said. "Now what?"

"I don't know," Holt began, "maybe we should just see what that noise is all about."

The two started toward the rumbling noise. The crunching of their footsteps echoed from tree to tree, and the woods began to take on a dream-like quality. A bluish haze drifted through the trees and lingered in the air. The noise came closer until it was just over the next hill.

"That sounds like artillery," said Wilson.

"Yeah, but it sounds different," replied Holt.

A light breeze ruffled the trees, and the smell of cordite stung their noses. The sounds of shouting and metal against metal seemed to fill the woods. Out of the corner of his eye Holt noticed a brown object lying under a bush. It was the same size as his map case and made of worn, cracked leather with a long strap. He picked it up and the black letters CSA jumped at him. Wilson took the case from him and examined it, but before he could ask a question a loud crashing noise came from behind them.

"Take cover!" Holt shouted.

From the direction they had just come, a team of horses pulling a cannon and limber exploded through the underbrush, trampling every sapling and bush in its path. A bearded man in a dirty gray uniform sat atop the limber shouting and cursing at the horses. His gray forage cap was pulled low over his eyes so that a black void filled the space just below the cap. From the opposite direction, a mounted rider charged up. He wore a gray coat that came just below his waist. His black boots came to his knees and were covered with mud.

"Take that cannon to the left flank!"

"Yes, sir!" yelled the driver, as he whipped the team into action.

Each man went his own way as the booming and exploding sounds continued from over the hill. Holt motioned to Wilson to follow as he headed for the crest.

At the top they looked down upon a mass of confusion. To their right a line of men in blue were moving forward, firing their muskets. To the left, men in gray were shooting at the advancing line. Cannon fire and exploding shells sent horses, dirt, and men catapulting into the air. Dirty smoke hung over the field like a heavy curtain. Stray bullets and fragments shook the bushes where Holt and Wilson hid. Suddenly, from the confusion of battle, a figure in a ragged gray uniform came running toward them. His eyes filled with terror. He stumbled over the rough ground, fell, got up and ran on. Out of the smoke, a horse carrying a soldier in blue came charging toward the man in gray. The horse and rider ran the man down and trampled him underfoot. The rider turned his horse and stood over the man. He pulled a pistol and fired three rounds into him, and then gallop back into the smoke and noise. After the rider left, Wilson sprang to his feet and sprinted to the fallen man.

"Wilson, come back here!"

Wilson reached the soldier and knelt beside him. Satisfied that he could do nothing for him, he started to run back to the hiding place. Abruptly, he stopped. His body jerked erect. A black hole had appeared in his forehead just above his nose. A small stream of blood flowed down his nose and dripped off the end. He pitched forward, twitched several times, and was still. Holt felt cold inside, even though he was sweating profusely. The noise and shouting of the battle was getting closer. Bullets a shell fragment now whined off the rocks and thudded into the trees around him. There was a slight movement behind him. He turned and saw two soldiers in blue staring at him. As they moved toward him, he leapt from his hiding place and ran to where Wilson lay

"Come on, Wilson! We gotta get out of here!

Wilson's dead eyes stared back.

"Come on! Say something! I don't want to leave you behind!"

Three dark spots of blood from Wilson's wound fell on Holt's hand. They hypnotized him, and he couldn't tear his eyes away from them. As he reached to brush them away, the force of a sledgehammer hit him in the middle of the back. He fell forward, and this time he couldn't smell the earth and leaves.

The Army waited three days for Sergeant Holt and Corporal Wilson to report. When they didn't, a search party was sent to find them. They found their gear hanging from a tree completely intact. They searched a twenty-mile radius from the gear looking for the two. One group found a cemetery with a monument erected to the men who had died in a battle of the Civil War. Surrounding the monument were neat rows of white crosses. On one cross was the inscription:

Killed in the Battle of Shiloh
April 7,1862
Corporal Daniel Wilson

On the next cross was the inscription:

Killed in the Battle of Shiloh
April 7, 1862
Sergeant Michael Holt

143

Chapter 18: Boilers

Written by Jean Trent

Canton, Ohio

May 17th, 1910

On a quiet street off Market Avenue, Nellie sat in the front room of her house, her feet crossed and not a hair out of place. She was a handsome woman of 24, normally high-spirited with a contagious laugh. She sat quietly plucking at a thread on her white cotton skirt. She knew something wasn't right – she woke up this morning with a knot in her stomach and Mabel had had one of her dreams, so Nellie was forewarned. Mable and Nellie were as close as two sisters could be. Mabel had the gift of intuition and she always knew when something was going to happen. Nellie could feel every beat of her heart in her chest.

Outside, she could hear people yelling and carts racing toward the southeast end of town -while inside, the annoying buzzing of a persistent fly that kept circling her was maddening. Mabel stepped outside onto the big front porch surrounded by substantial brick railings. Neighbors and friends were quickly gathering, speaking in low voices. There were hushed whispers of boilers and talk of an explosion.

~

Reginald materialized with a start. "Confound it!" He yelled. The last thing he remembered was that damned high-

144

pitched buzzing. And now he was here in this mess. The buzzing was replaced by screams, men yelling and women sobbing in the distance. Dust and smoke made it difficult to get his bearings. "This can't be good."

"Come on, man! If you're not injured, you must dig!" PV McLean grabbed Reginald by the shirt sleeve and yanked him toward the pile of rubble that had once been a tin plate factory.

"There were over a hundred men in this plant – now move!" The man's voice was loud and stern. The smell of smoke and flesh wound its way into Reginald's nostrils.

"Where am I?" asked Reginald.

"No time for questions," boomed PV's voice. Reginald pulled up his sleeves and dove into the debris pile.

I will figure out when and where later – no time for trivialities right now. He thought to himself.

Reginald dug for what felt like hours, and he was not used to this kind of work. He came from a sturdy Irish family of factory workers, but his mother always pampered and spoiled him – keeping her baby away from the brashness of manual labor. Reginald was experiencing manual labor now. His delicate hands were pinched, smashed, and cut. His blood mixed with ash and sweat, and dirt rolled down his forehead to his eyes. Finally he saw what he thought was the fingers of a hand. They were distorted and mangled. He became excited over his find and frantically started digging. It was a hand – but only a hand. Reginald dropped it like a hot potato and promptly turned his head to vomit his breakfast he had with Dottie that morning– (when was that? A few decades ago?) - all over a pile of steel and brick.

145

The hot sun burned the back of his neck and hands as they continued digging and moving rubble. He soon found what he thought was a boot and started digging frantically and timidly at the same time, afraid of what he might find. Yes, there was a leg, two legs were soon uncovered. He gingerly proceeded but P.V. was digging in the area where the rest of the torso might be, should it still be attached to the body. At this time, another man joined them and started digging as he was asking about his brother, Harry, who he had been searching for amid the rubble. Harry was nowhere to be found.

The flurry of digging continued: legs led to hips, torso, and head – all connected, made up one young man who was lifeless under all that rubble. P.V. and Reginald stood up. Milton knelt on the ground and wrapped his arms around his young brother. There was no breath, no glint of orneriness in his eyes. He was gone. Milton couldn't suck breath in or get air out. How was he still here and his brother gone? How would he tell his mother? How would he tell Nellie? He knew one thing: Harry was going home with him.

~

Nellie sat in the parlor, a slight breeze blowing. She still hadn't moved. She could hear the birds singing and the rustle of the leaves and the ticking of the clock on the mantle. A few flies buzzed around, then everything stopped. This was the calm before the storm mama had often referred to. This wouldn't be her first, and unfortunately not her last. She heard the clumping of the horse hooves against the brick road. They were loud and hollow today. She heard the squeaking and rattling of the carriage wheels – every turn of them. And when they stopped, they stopped too close. She heard the soft voices of men and one that was unrecognizable. She heard Mabel take in a deep breath and let out a quiet sob. She heard the steps on the stairs up the porch and she herself took a deep breath, squared her shoulders, and sat up straight. She would face this head on, she told herself.

Milton was the first to come in through screen door, gently pulling Mabel alongside him. Then P.V. – Nellie knew P.V., and then another man came in who she did not recognize. All three men were covered in dirt, sweat, and blood, all holding their hats in their hands, heads bowed, except for Milton. He met her gaze. She took another breath. She had to think about it now. She squared her jaw. Milton knelt before her and took her small hands in his.

"Nellie, he's gone, he's gone – I'm so sorry, he's gone," tears crept down his cheeks. "I brought him with me – I didn't know where else to bring him." The only sound in the room was the clock on the mantel. Tick-tock-tick-tock. It echoed against the wood. Nellie heard her voice choke out of her throat, as if someone was speaking for her.

"You did the right thing, Milton. Now there is work to be done; we must clear off the table and put a blanket down. He needs to be cleaned up. Bring him in." P.V. and Milton promptly went outside to do so.

Reginald had never dealt with death before and couldn't help but admire this beautiful woman's strong stance with such devastating news. He could see the glistening of a tear, which Nellie discreetly wiped away. He watched her quietly as she settled herself and prepared the dining room table, covering it carefully with a blanket. He moved a little closer.

"I'm so sorry for your loss, Ma'am.' Usually quite cocky, he now stuttered over his words. "Is there anything I can do to help?"

Nellie jutted her chin out again and simply stated "The pan – in the sideboard by the stove – get it and fill it with water; I will get the towels and soap." She knew this would be the most difficult thing for her to do but it would be one of the last times she would be with the love of her life. Reginald fumbled with the pan careful not to spill the water and brought it into the room. When he sat the pan down, he heard a buzzing. Nellie hear it too.

"Get that fly out of here! If you want to help you will get rid of that fly." She turned her attention to the front door, took a deep breath, turned her head, and the man and the fly were gone.

Nellie was a strong woman, but Harry was the one true love of her life, and as the days, weeks, and months following that fateful day passed, they became a blur for Nellie. The time was filled with whispering visitors all too eager to impart their words of wisdom, and the tick-tock of the mantel clock. The plant did not reopen and eventually the remains of the factory were leveled, and a different factory was built in its place.

One day, many months later something happened which was a turning point in her life. Momma, Mabel, and Nellie were sitting at the kitchen table snapping beans when Nellie heard the sound of a buzzing fly which brought back a flood of memories and emotions. Chaos immediately ensued.

As the fly flew across the room, mittens, the cat, dove after it, jumping and swatting. When mamma got up to open the door to shoo the fly out, a black Labrador barreled into the kitchen after mittens, who was still chasing the fly. The fly then flew across the kitchen table with mittens right behind it, and the black lab was on the cat's tail – running across the kitchen table. Beans flew everywhere. Mamma, Nellie, and

Mabel went spinning and ducking trying to catch the beans. As quick as it started, the fly, the cat, and the dog went out the door.

The three ladies looked at each other and the mess. Mama started out with a quiet chuckle, which turned into a combined roar with all three ladies doubled over in laugher. For the first time in over a year, Nellie truly laughed.

There was a knock at the door. The women composed themselves as Nellie went to answer it. Much to her surprise, it was the man she had only seen once before who had disappeared so quickly. He was standing outside the door talking to himself – holding his hat in one hand and a leash with the black Lab in the other. With the buzzing of a fly, Reginald found himself once again outside of Miss Nellie's home.

"Darn fly! How did that dang thing manage to drag that dog with me this time?" Reginald muttered as he frantically attempted to compose himself. He had been dog-sitting Thomas's newest acquisition in an attempt to keep this cat-hungry mutt that had been left with Thomas away from Cora the cat. This was supposed to be a temporary situation. But now – here he was transported in time with the dog.

He was startled by the opening of the screen door and a soft familiar face observing his lack of composure with what seemed to be a glimmer of laughter in her beautiful blue eyes. He had to think fast.

"Ma'am I am so sorry to bother you – I just want to apologize for this dog's behavior and to offer any help I may in cleaning up." Reginald stuttered his way through the sentence. *Confound it! Compose yourself, man!* He thought to himself.

149

Nellie looked beautiful; this was not the heartbroken, stoic woman he had remembered. She scolded Reginald.

"Why sir, don't you know how to control that mutt? There are beans from here to Timbuktu!" Reginald once again was at a loss for words. This young woman was one of very few people who had that effect on him. He quietly hung his head and muttered.

"I was dog-sitting this lab for a friend and he kind of got away from me. I'm terribly sorry."

"Well, it looks like you have him a bit under control now. Would you like some ice cool lemonade?" Nellie took pity on him and assumed the flush on his face was from the heat – it was hot for late June.

Reginald replied quickly. "Yes Ma'am!" By this time Mama and Mabel had joined Reginald on the broad front porch and they offered him a seat on one of the green wicker chairs. There was a light summer breeze in the air. All three women were a little ruffled by the ordeal; normally meticulously pinned hair on all three was disheveled. Mama offered the gentleman a bushel of beans to start snapping and invited him to dinner. Secretly, mama was delighted to serve this man dinner. Because of his black lab, her sweet Nellie had laughed again, and the heaviness of the past year seemed to have been lifted from her. Mama drew in a great sigh of relief. She knew her daughter would be ok.

The years went by and Nellie would see Reginald every now and then. He would pop in and out of her life at the oddest times, and each was preceded by the sound of a buzzing fly. It seemed to appear just before he arrived and right before he left. Despite Reginald's odd appearances and disappearances, they grew to be friends.

Chapter 19: Forwards from Backward

Written by Benjamin Dine

Finland

1933

It was a cool night during the summertime in 1933. Edward Smith and his partner, Elizabeth Moore, were outside in a wetland near Oulu, Finland during the midnight sun. The twenty-eight-year-old Edward was a British gentleman from a wealthy family. He had short brown hair and deep blue eyes. He was a bit bulky, but not rotund.

His partner and fiancé, Elizabeth, who was twenty-six, had curly blonde hair and blue eyes. She had a lithe build to her frame and was the apple of Edward's eyes.

"My dear Edward, why do we have to be out so late?" Elizabeth asked. "It is close to midnight."

"I believe I can get some extra work done," the geologist replied. "I want to get to the bottom of this bizarre phenomenon of this lake before us; it's constantly frozen despite the rest of this wetland being thawed out."

"I do remember that you have trouble sleeping and the midnight sun isn't going to help you with that," Elizabeth answered in concern.

"I have to do this," Edward stated. "The scientific expo is coming up within a week and I need to find the discovery of the century." The woman threw her arms up and sighed.

151

"Here you go again with your competitive streak," Elizabeth replied. The geologist then went up to the frozen lake. He knelt down to examine it until he spotted something unusual in the lakebed.

"What do we have here?" He asked. "I see something at the bottom." He pointed it out to his fiancé.

"What is it? A shiny stone?" She asked.

"Don't be sooty. It looks like some kind of item," he said, his interest sparked. "I'm no anthropologist but I think we should try to get it out." He grabbed his pickaxe and started to pick at the ice. "Come on, Elizabeth. Can you give me a hand here?"

"Alright." She grabbed a pickaxe and started to pick away at the ice with her fiancé. The ice began to crack and buckle under their weight.

"MOVE!!" He shouted. The two were at least able to move quick enough to not sink into the water as the ice busted apart. The chunks began to float about the lake's surface. They looked back into where they had cracked the ice. They could see that item more clearly. "It looks like some kind of artifact."

"That doesn't look like any artifact I know of," Elizabeth replied.

"Perhaps, we should fish it out," Edward answered.

After grabbing some rope and tying it around his waist, Edward dove into the brine. He found the artifact from within the muddy bottom and pulled it out. He returned to the surface and gave it to Elizabeth to analyze.

The base of the silver artifact was the size of a dinner plate. The moon phases were printed along the copper rim of

the artifact. In the center, attached to the base, was a cylinder two soda cans thick and tall. The sides were decorated with brass waterfowl. On the top was a series of metal wires coming from the center curling upwards and over the cylinder. At the end of each wire, there was a colored ornament made from gold. Each one shaped like a bear.

"This is a very peculiar artifact," she stated, confused. "I have no clue what this could be."

"My question is... how does it work?" He asked her.

"Please be patient, dear Edward," Elizabeth rebuked. "I don't even know what it does." She looked at the interesting piece of equipment. Elizabeth grabbed onto one of the bears and decide to push it to a different location.

They heard a loud high-pitched buzzing sound coming from the device she was holding. The duo felt their bodies tremble as if being twisted.

"What's going on here?" Edward asked.

"Is it this artifact doing it or the timeflies again?" Elizabeth asked.

"IN ANY CASE, SHUT IT OFF!" He shouted. She tried to reach for the moved bear. However, it seemed to slow down and stop on its own. They both sighed in relief as their bodies returned to normal. "Let's not do that again."

"Agreed," she answered. The two of them looked around.

"Wait, where is our gear?" Edward asked in scared surprise.

"Forget about the gear, where's Oulu?" She answered. They looked towards the city's location and there was no city to be found only the taiga forest of conifers remained. They gazed upward and still noticed the midnight sun in the sky.

"We must be in the past again," he stated in shock.

"But how far back are we?" she asked.

"From the looks of things...", he stated in a panic. "the very distant past." At that moment, they heard the sounds of howling wolves. "Wolves here?"

"Okay, let's stay calm and hope we don't get spotted," Edward commented. The duo trekked across the taiga forest in an attempt to find anything resembling a town or village for that matter. They found no village, but they eventually found a structure. "What in the world is that?"

They had spotted a cottage on stilts, but they saw that the supported building was upside-down. They looked intently at the structure trying to make sense of it.

"The supports are made from steel!?" Elizabeth asked. "How is this possible?" In addition, they saw that most of the structure was made from various metals. They had noticed some scrap metal on the ground near the structure's base. "What could have created such a thing?"

"No, that doesn't work." A voice was heard saying. Then, they saw a piece of metal fly out of the window of the structure for a little bit it started to fall upward before falling to the ground.

"Uh... excuse me," Edward stated.

"Huh? Who's there?" The eccentric-sounding voice added. It was a moment later, they saw a bearded man look out of the window. He had shaggy brown hair and blue eyes, though he appeared upside down in the window. "Oh, I have visitors. Hold on a second." He went back into the structure.

They saw the stilts extend to lift the cottage. The building turned right side up and landed back on the ground with the front door facing them. Then, the man came out of the door. They noticed he was quite tall for people in the region. And from what he was wearing, they could tell that the stranger was a smith by craft.

"Hello," the man stated. "Welcome to my home." The two people just looked at each other for a moment and then back to the man.

"Thanks," Elizabeth replied.

"What are you hearing?" The guy asked.

"I'm listening to you," Edward replied.

"No... are you doing well?" The eccentric man asked.

"No, we're a bit lost,." Elizabeth replied.

"Who are you anyway?" Edward asked him, baffled at the sight of the eccentric male.

"Oh you must not be from these parts," he said. "My name is Ilmarinen."

"Ilmarinen... why does that name sound so familiar?" Elizabeth asked herself, thinking for a moment. "As a historian,

I should know what something like that is."

"What brings you here?" The craft smith asked the two of them.

"We came here accidently," she said.

"What do you mean accidently?" Ilmarinen replied. "No one comes to a place by accident. There must be a reason why you came to my doorstep."

"We are looking for Oulu." Edward answered.

"What kind of trinket is an Oulu?" He replied.

"It's a place, not an item," the man stated.

"I've never heard of this place called Oulu," Ilmarinen replied. "Is it a nice place?" Edward just slapped his forehead at this.

"Is this a joke?" Edward asked once again. "You live here. You must really be pulling the biggest bluff I've ever heard."

"What if he isn't bluffing, dear Edward?" Elizabeth asked her fiancé. "What if he truly doesn't know where Oulu is?"

"I don't know what to say," he replied to her.

"I don't know where Oulu city is," Ilmarinen stated to them. "Then again, I can't find my own head most of the time. Did you travel far?"

"Well..." Elizabeth explained. "Not exactly, we found this thing in a frozen swamp. We messed with it and found our way here."

"What are you talking about?" The smith asked. She held up the metal object to the smith. His eyes went wide, and a smile appeared on his face.

"Oh, you found my aikalentää," he answered.

"A what?" Edward asked. "I'm not a linguist."

"You found the timefly seeker I built," the smith explained.

"A timefly seeker?" Elizabeth asked him still confused. "You made this? But I thought – "

"It's a trinket that allows you to track timeflies wherever they may be," Ilmarinen explained. "It's the most useless thing I have ever created."

"You built a timefly seeker," Edward answered, a look of annoyance appearing on his face. "How is that useless?! It's one of the most useful things one can create."

"Timeflies don't exist anymore," Ilmarinen said.

"What do you mean, don't exist anymore?" Edward asked.

"As far as I know, they were wiped out by Vainamoinen," the smith stated.

"Okay. So, do you know how to operate the tracker?" Elizabeth asked.

"I built the trinket, yes," the smith replied. "But I never tested it, so I don't even know if it actually works because I misplaced it. But I thank you for returning it to me nonetheless." He fiddled with the levers and the designs shifted. They pointed to an area of space that was empty.

"Well, it's a bust," Ilmarinen replied as he handed back the device. "I'm heading back to work." He left the room.

The two people went to the spot where the device had pointed. Then as they stopped in the spot for a few seconds. The normal reaction of the timeflies occurred with them and the device. They disappeared. Ilmarinen returned to the room.

"Huh?" He asked looking around. "Where did they go?"

Edward and Elizabeth returned back to the time they were once in. They looked around and saw everything was in place.

"I'm glad we're back in our time once again," Elizabeth said.
"I guess this device really can track the areas of space a timefly has been," Edward replied. "But what's surprising is that those areas seem empty. Yet this seeker is able to detect the timefly's presence. I want to figure out how this thing works."

"But something still gets me though, dear Edward," the woman asked.

"What's that?" He asked.

"Ilmarinen had stated that it was the useless thing he created because the timeflies no longer exist. Yet we are dealing with them now." Elizabeth said. "This is starting to get very creepy. What exactly are these timeflies? Are they some kind of anomaly?"

"Elizabeth, we will find out sooner or later," Edward answered. "But in any case, at least we have the Seeker to help us with that."

Chapter 20: The Return of Time
Written by Mela Saylor

Jackson Township
1921

Dottie rematerialized with a popping noise this time, sounding as though she was being pushed into this new dimension. Recognizing the landscape, she knew she was back in 1921 – thank goodness. The sun hadn't begun to set yet and Dottie took off running through the cornfields to find Reginald and Thomas, having no idea where or when they were. The corn was still high, and she could hear cicadas, certain it was still August. So much had happened to her it seemed she was gone much longer.

Hoping she was going in the right direction, she kept jumping up trying to look over the stalks of corn towering over her head. *Couldn't I have just materialized in front of the clock shop?* she thought to herself.

When she stopped to catch her breath and leaned over, hands on her knees, she noticed her locket was gone. Where could that have gotten lost – or rather, when? An unexpected cold breeze rustled through the corn stalks and snaked around her. She shivered and started running again like the devil was on her tail.

Ten minutes later finding the rise of land where they first sighted the shop, she jumped up trying to see if it was there. It was. The sun was resting on the horizon and from the east nightfall was creeping up behind her bringing with it strong winds.

By the time she reached the clock shop, she stopped to catch her breath by the door, then vigorously knocked. The door flew open and multiple hands reached out to drag her inside. The door slammed shut behind her. Someone threw the dead bolt. They were all there, thank goodness, she thought, as they formed a circle around and peppered her with questions.

"Where've you been?"

"Are you alright?"

"What happened?"

"Do you **HAVE** it?"

The questions all came at once. She held out her hand, placing it on Reginald's shoulder, steadying herself and gave a shaky smile.

"I don't have it, but I know where you put it – or where you will put it in the future. I don't know if this makes any sense, but because of the timeflies, time has become, or will become fluid. In the future it speeds up, slows down, and goes in reverse at whim. So we've got to take care of this right now."

The wind started picking up outside, rattling the door in its frame, startling everyone. Dorothy strode outside the circle of her friends and Thomas and went to the side desk Thomas from 2020 had shown her. She turned it around and groped in the back for its secret compartment.

"How about that?" Thomas scratched himself on the head. "I don't remember doing that."

"Don't worry – if we're lucky you'll never do this in about ninety-nine years." Dorothy brought the small instrument out of its hiding place and showed it to everyone. They all stared. Thomas was the first to speak.

"What the heck is that? And what the blazes am I supposed to do with that –play those damned flies a tune?" Dorothy smiled. She had to speak up to be heard over the clatter the wind was making on the shop.

"It's the IV Frequency Meter you made in 2020.

"IV Frequency Meter?"

"It stands for Internal Vibrational Frequency. I think you blow on it somehow – my brain is fried right now – I just don't know which hole you blow into." She turned the small instrument over in her hands looking for some indication of how this was to be used.

"And then what?"

"I don't know – you didn't have time to tell me – that place was a mess."

"My shop?" Thomas's voice rose an octave.

"No – the time. Time wasn't cooperating with anyone. It became an unpredictable entity – very fluid - so no one knew what time it was – everything was amok." They all looked at her in surprise.

"The world was falling apart."

"Ohhh," everyone around her said in unison.

"Oh let's just get on with it." Thomas grabbed the IVF meter out of her hands and blew on it. He scowled and handed it back to her.

"Doesn't work."

"That can't be – it's never been used before."

Edward grabbed it.

"Let me see." He turned it over and blew into a different opening. Still nothing.

And as they were passing the innocuous looking instrument back and forth, the wind was doing its best to get into that shop. Elizabeth, standing by the window, came over to the men and laid her hand over the instrument, stopping them from any further damage.

"Perhaps it's like a dog whistle – only the flies can hear it."

"Ohhh!" was heard from all.

The wind stopped immediately, and the instant silence brought the five people in the clock shop to quiet themselves.

"Just listen," Elizabeth whispered. "do you hear that?"

In the distance a humming sound could be heard. Faintly at first, but it soon became louder and the minutes on all Thomas's clocks started ticking again from the time they left off at – 8:20 pm.

"The clocks have started again!"

"That means it's working!"

"Um, Reggie," Edward whispered in the growing din, "you're the bug expert – "

"Entomologist," he corrected.

"Ok- if two bugs started reproducing now, in 1921, how many would there be by the year 2020?"

"Easily in the millions, billions, probably trillions, if not more." Reginald's eyes were dancing with merriment as he passed on this information and he winked at Elizabeth. The humming sound of a legion wings filled the sky. Elizabeth blanched, and worriedly Thomas looked heavenward.

"This doesn't sound good." He raised his voice over the din outside, "Jonas –Do you hear me? They're all here and we're coming back now!"

"So where are they going?" Elizabeth placed her hand on her throat and began to hyperventilate.

"I daresay they are coming here to see me," Thomas grinned.

And the moment Thomas said that, the windows began to shudder with the impact of the insects, all needing to get in. The shop darkened with generations tenfold of the timeflies blocking every window. And then they were vibrating with their humming. Their bodies pulsed and glowed with a luminous purple-white light. The wind howled outside while the five people inside clutched each other and stared at the glowing insects. Dottie was the first to break their silence.

"Now what?"

"I guess we go back the way we came – the timeflies and myself." Thomas looked excited at the prospect. He looked around the shop, then patted Elizabeth's hand.

"I have to let them in, dear."

The vibrations from the shop itself began so slowly they weren't immediately noticeable with all the commotion of the insects and the wind outside. Edward was the first to notice the floorboards rattling.

"Hey, Reggie –is it just me or is this floor vibrating?"

Reginald and Dottie looked at each other, their mouths opening in surprise when they realized what was about to happen, and said at the same time,

"We've got to get out of here now!"

"While they're trying to get in? Nooooo!" Elizabeth wailed, burrowing her head in Edwards arms and sobbing. "It's my nightmare all over again!"

"Shhh! Everything will be fine, but we've got to get out of here or we'll end up stuck forty some years into the future – in a different country! One quick run for it, ok?' Dottie stroked Elizabeth on her shoulders and Elizabeth cried even harder in Edward's arms. Dottie looked at Edward.

"You have to get her out of here – if you have to carry her."

"I know. We'll be right behind you". Edward grimaced at the thought of fighting their way out through the swarm.

~~~

The outside door was almost impossible to open. It took all the strength Reginald and Dottie had. The insects had plastered themselves over every part of the building by now – at least a foot deep in some places – and the outside door was one of them. But once pried open an inch, their weight on the door dissipated as they all poured into the building hitting Reginald and Dottie full force and knocking them over. They were in the middle of an enormous swarm and Dottie tried to grab Reginald's hand to find her way out. Instead, she found his hand covered with the timeflies and ended up getting bitten several times. But he was there, and she got on her knees and started crawling in his direction, head down. The swarm darkened the interior, but at the same time, lit it up with their tiny pulsating lights they emitted from their hind quarters. The affect the flies had on the humans with their lights and their humming was disorienting. Dottie couldn't see anything as she was in the middle of the swarm, she hoped it was the middle. There were so many, and she kept getting hit with them as she tried to crawl through that. She kept moving forward until she started breathing fresh air. She opened her eyes a crack. Edward was ten feet ahead of her sprawled on the ground on top of some broken corn stalks. When she crawled over to him to give him a hug, he grabbed her by the hair and pulled out a time fly that had gotten entangled in it. He threw it in the air, and they watched it turn around and fly into the shop.

"Where's Elizabeth and Edward?" Dottie broke their silence, her voice shaky.

"Give them a few more moments – I'm sure they'll make it out." Reginald had no plans to go back in shop. Was there even standing room in there? He wondered how packed the shop was at this point.

Just then the shop blinked and disappeared then reappeared with a rumbling.

"Oh no, Reggie!" Dottie reached out to touch him.

"Look! There they are." Relief flooded into Reginald's voice as he gave a big sigh.

Edward came out stumbling through the door with Elizabeth in his arms. He fell down the step into the cornfield and they laid there, stunned.

For one brief second, they saw the shop shudder and heard the timeflies screeching inside. The shop flickered one last time and disappeared completely, leaving a slowly dispersing cloud of smoke in its wake.

The four of them lay there on their backs in the cornfield, stunned by the absence of the shop and the silence of the night. Slowly the night creatures came to life around them again. They heard bullfrogs and peepers in the distance.

Elizabeth raised her hand to her head.

"My head hurts."

"Did all that really happen?" Reginald wondered out loud.

"That was some strong applejack if it didn't." Edward laughed nervously., swatting away a mosquito.

A few shooting stars passed by overhead, drawing their attention to the night sky. Dottie gasped as she looked above her.

"Oh no – look at that!" What they saw above them in the night sky were trillions more timeflies that didn't make it back to the clock shop before it disappeared. They were still coming back from the future and the past.

The timeflies returned from the far reaches of time the same way they went but this time they returned as a force to be reckoned with, meeting in the sky, joining, and moving together as one continuous entity with one mind and one body illuminating the night. Their murmuration took the shape of a snake. There was no end in sight to this spectacle and they came at a speed that compressed their magic bodies together. After ten minutes of this, they became dust and finally their twinkling disappeared from sight.

"Wow. I guess Thomas is back in 1961 now, right?" Reginald sat up from his prone position, rubbing his neck where the crushed corn stalks had jabbed him. Elizabeth sat up quickly realizing that her little companion was now gone.

"Cora! The cat was still in the shop when it left here! Oh no!"

"I'm sure Thomas will take care of it." Dottie said absentmindedly, her mind on Vincent.

"Guys let's just get out of here now and not say a word to anyone about what happened. Okay? We've our reputations to think about." Edward said, still dusting himself off. Reginald grinned.

"No one would believe us anyway. Oh, I say, shhh! Look." Reginald held a finger to his lips, then pointed to an owl he had been observing. It screeched as it made a lunge for a small field mouse it was stalking. The owl crossed paths with where the last of the timeflies had been before they vanished. The owl and the mouse disappeared.

Chapter 21: Norway at Midnight 1961

It was almost midnight when Jonas heard a crashing sound in his shop below.

"I'm coming! I'm coming!" he grumbled as he threw on a robe and grabbed the lantern sitting on his night table. In his haste he hobbled down the creaky wooden stairs to the first floor in his bare feet.

"This is why I can't get any sleep around here," he grumbled. "Something's always coming or going." More noise ensued. There was crashing and screeching—and sneezing coming from the backroom.

"Oh dammit, Pandora! No more problems, I swear!" But when Jonas finally opened the door to the backroom, he saw the clock shop he created to send Thomas to, encased in a huge bubble filling up the entirety of the cave-like room. There were a few million timeflies swarming inside it with Thomas.

Thomas was standing just outside the shop, still encased in the bubble, sneezing, his eyes red and tearing up.

166

"Aaah-ahh-achoo!-achoo!"

"Great Zeus!" Jonas backed away slightly from the bubble. "What happened? Thomas – can you see me?" he shouted.

Thomas slowly opened his red-rimmed eyes and scowled at Jonas.

"Do you have any idea what I had to endure on my way back here? Those flying pests of yours have reproduced out the whazoo and they were wrapped so tightly around me I could hardly breathe on the way back. Is your demon gone yet? Please tell me this is 1961."

"Right – right – right, of course it is. Relax, you've only been gone for a week." Jonas looked around the place trying to figure out what to do with the excessive amount of timeflies that were swarming inside this bubble. It wouldn't do for them to be loose in the shop – and he certainly couldn't have Demonico getting his hands on any one of them. This was a definite problem. He had to hide them- and fast. And inside the clock shop he heard all the clocks ticking once more. That gave him an idea.

"I see you got the time right – it's all working right again."

"Finally – and it took 57 years on my end to get it right. Thomas glared at him as he took a swipe at one of the flies attempting to land on him. "Damn things. You could have TOLD me I had to MAKE that IV Meter." he muttered.

"Don't touch the sides of this!" Jonas shouted.

"What's it gonna do?"

"I don't know, but I can't let those flies get out of that bubble."

"So DO something! Aren't you a wizard? Conjure something -do whatever wizards do!"

Jonas held up his hands – palms facing the enormous bubble that sat at a tilt in this cave-like structure. He closed his eyes tightly.

"Ah –" Thomas contorted his face.

"Shh! Let me concentrate!" Then he began:

"Trick, trock the restarted clocks

Pillars of time, embrace your new housing,

Forwards, backwards,

Infinitum to infinity.

Trick the trock, tic-toc – BUBBLE POP!"

As Jonas uttered the last syllable, the timeflies vanished with the bubble.

"Where'd they go?" Thomas stood there with his mouth open.

"Into your clocks," Jonas yawned.

Thomas turned around and looked into the clock shop.

"They're all contained? All of them?"

"Yes. Look around you. Not one last insect."

"What about the rest of them?"

"The rest?"

"Uh, yeah – the shop disappeared before they all came back, I'm positive of that."

"Whoa!" Jonas had to sit down to process that. Thomas followed him into the outer shop.

Jonas gave a big sigh. "Looks like I've done it again."

"Done what?"

By this time both Jonas and Thomas had wandered to the front and sat down at a corner table. Jonas grabbed a bottle of whisky from under the front counter and sat down. After pouring drinks, he handed one to Thomas.

"The Old Ones have cursed me with collateral magic every time I cast a spell."

"What do you mean by 'collateral magic'?"

"Unintended consequences of any and all magic I use."

"And these last two spells?"

"We shall see in good time. Right now, it looks like the collateral implications of the return spell's parameters weren't large enough to accommodate all those problematic insects." Jonas poured them each another drink.

"Here – this ought to cure what ails you." He passed it to Thomas.

"Oh, my head hurts." Thomas leaned back in his chair and closed his eyes.

Jonas closed his eyes also, hoping to get a few hours sleep before morning but was jolted awake when Thomas gasped aloud and wide-eyed, jumped out of his seat.

"What the devil has got into you?"

"I – I – closed my eyes and saw something!" Thomas started pacing back and forth in front of Jonas trying to make sense of what he saw.

"And I'd like to see the inside of my eyelids," Jonas curtly replied. "Have you been drinking or something?"

"No! Yes! But it was so real. When I closed my eyes, I felt as if I was in the middle of something awful. I could hear things too. There was an explosion, people were hurt and killed. I smelled the fires!" Thomas pounded his fist on the table and brought his face up to Jonas. Thomas finally sat back down across from Jonas, albeit a bit wide eyed. And then Jonas looked at Thomas.

"What color are your eyes?"

"Blue. Why?" Why the change in subject, Thomas wondered.

"That's what I thought. They're not blue now – your eyes are a metallic silver." Jonas got up and came closer to Thomas and peered into his eyes. "Oh no."

"Why? What? Do you see something?" Thomas was too rattled now to do any sleeping.

"I have a feeling you may have had the timeflies' magic rubbed all over you, and into your eyes, on the way back here. They may have given you second sight. That's one explanation."

"And another explanation?"

"You've been drinking."

And just then a cat jumped on the table between the two men, startling them.

"Where'd this cat come from?" Jonas had a bad history with cats and didn't like them at all, not since his first medium, Dierdre, turned on him to the Old Ones.

"This cat? I've no idea. The girls picked up a stray in 1921 and brought it to the shop with them. But that's not Cora."

"You named the girl's cat?" Jonas raised his white bushy eyebrows in surprise. Thomas blushed.

"We've been together for a while."

The cat arched her back on the table between the two men and, purring loudly, rubbed herself against Thomas. She eyed Jonas with suspicion. Jonas saw that its coat was a silvery white. He looked from the cat to Thomas's eyes.

"Oh crap."

"What?"

"I've got news for you - this IS your Cora. This cat obviously came through time with you. Who knows what it has or is now or the extent of its magic powers – and let's hope to god it doesn't have any. It's got to stay with me to prevent god knows what."

And then the two men heard the clocks in the clock shop. They had all recalibrated and their ticking was as one. It sounded like a human heartbeat WUMP – WUMP – WUMP! Both men jumped up and went running to the backroom.

"Will this night ever end?" Jonas was getting too old for this crap.

When they got to the open door of the backroom the clock shop was vibrating.

What is going on?" Thomas shouted, trying to be heard over the din of the clocks inside and the shop itself.

"I'm guessing that the remaining timeflies created a wormhole of sorts and it's getting pretty darn close to the shop for it to be vibrating like this!"

Then they saw them – more timeflies came out of the shop toward Thomas and flew around him, encasing him in a gelatinous bubble. As he was being dragged back into the heart of the beating clock shop he shouted to Jonas.

"What's going on? Where are they taking me? Jonas retreated to the safety of the outer shop and watched the flies and the clocks reclaim his new friend.

"I don't know – but you have those clocks now – use them to your advantage!"

"What? How?"

"You can adjust time now – use it to your advantage, you know you can change – "

Before Jonas could finish the sentence, Thomas and the clock shop disappeared once more from the back room. The silence was deafening.

"Oh, crap."

Algiers

1942

Somewhere in time a "boom" sounded in the heavens and an unassuming clock shop appeared on the side of a mountain in an arid region. Thomas tentatively opened his door to the sound of drums and smelled smoke rising in the distance. He fell on his knees in disbelief, yelling to the sky.

"Jonas, NOOOO! Not again!"
He ran into the shop and began tearing it apart clock by ticking clock.   ~~~

About the Greater Canton Writers' Guild

The Greater Canton Writers' Guild was founded in 1964 for beginning and professional writers for purposes of learning, discussion, and mutual support. It includes persons of diverse skills who share a common commitment to the craft of writing.

From the beginning, exchanges of ideas, manuscript critiques, and reports of market information have produced lively and informative monthly meetings. Friendships have formed, and poetry, short stories, and books have emerged.

Guild meetings are open to anyone who has an interest in writing. Please join us at our next meeting and bring a writing friend! You can find out about our meetings on our website and on Facebook.

About our authors…

William Alford is a native of Virginia with degrees in Journalism from Marshall University and Industrial Design from the University of Cincinnati. With thirty US and International patents, William has transitioned his creativity into writing fiction. He is the proud recipient of the 2014 Marlene Stottsberry Award for fiction.

Eleni Byrnes was VP of the Writers Guild for several years. She has led poetry workshops and served as a judge for Ohio Poetry Day. Much of her inspiration is derived from nature and spirituality. With a background rooted in poetry, a love of words and vernacular, nestled within these pages is her first published story.

Benjamin Dine is a Kent State University graduate who writes fiction and is a published poet. He is also a gamer and Dungeon Master who creates artwork.

Ed Klink lived in the skies as a private pilot for 32 years and in his imagination ever since. An avid historian, he has been writing historical fiction since he retired in 2012. He is a graduate of Master Class by James Patterson, and a member of the Greater Canton Writers' Guild, and the Shepherd's Quill. You can find some of his writing on his blog, edwardklink.blogspot.com.

Ron Luikart, a veteran of the Viet Nam War, is a retired teacher who taught writing and American Literature at Jackson Local for 31 years. Currently he is working as an adjunct professor at Kent State University. A recipient of the Stottsberry and Ken Miller Awards, he favors the short story.

Mela Saylor started out studying journalism and ended up with a bachelor's in art and education. Her writing, published in several newspapers, magazines, and periodicals, slowly transitioned to fiction where she focuses on writers and artists and their relationships with the mediums they use. She has a blog http://paintandpens.blogspot.com where she explores matters of art, writing, and creativity. Except for a brief hiatus, she has served as president of the Guild since 2009.

Caroline Burry Totten is a Canton native. A former reporter, she has published sixty-five short stories, many articles, poems, and two books. She is a charter member of the Greater Canton Writer's Guild and the founder of the Midwest Writers' Conference.

Jean Trent is a paramedic firefighter living her dream in the city she grew up in. She has combined her love of writing and photography in a blog about her adventures. Through images and words, she tells her stories. She is currently working on a novella which seems to be in a constant state of metamorphosis. Jean serves as vice president of the Greater Canton Writers' Guild.

About the 8:20 Clock...

The clock on the back cover was manufactured by the Wm L. Gilbert Clock Company in Winsted, Connecticut around 1877. The two holes on the face of this clock, one at the eight and the other at the four, are where keys are inserted to wind it, hence the name 8:20 Clock Shop.

Mr. Jack Hood, the owner of the 8:20 Clock Shop, was kind enough to let me photograph the clocks for this project. He first began working on clocks at 8 years of age in Pittsburgh, PA.

At that time, when the three rivers that converged in Pittsburgh overflowed their banks, the shopkeepers whose property flooded, threw their goods out into gondolas, (coal cars). Mr. Hood's father, who also worked at the railroad, would bring some of these items back to his own shop and the young Jack Hood would open them out of curiosity as to their inner workings. His curiosity and fascination with clocks became a lifelong career.

The 8:20 Clock Shop has been at its current location at 5870 Fulton Drive since 1983. He repairs clocks and watches and sells vintage cameras and clocks.

By Jean Trent,
Beyond the Images Photography